Village Affairs

THREE'S COMPANY

KRISTIAN PARKER

Three's Company
ISBN # 978-1-80250-978-6
©Copyright Kristian Parker 2022
Cover Art by Kelly Martin ©Copyright September 2022
Interior text design by Claire Siemaszkiewicz
Pride Publishing

Published in 2022 by Pride Publishing, United Kingdom.

Pride Publishing is an imprint of Totally Entwined Group Limited.

Pride Publishing books by Kristian Parker

Speak Its Name
To Light a Fire
Call it Love
Spotlight on Love

Village Affairs
The Rule of Three
Three's Company

Collections
My Bloody Valentine: Venetian Valentine
Sun, Sea and Spotted Squid

THREE'S COMPANY

Dedication

To my Satinder. My partner in crime with the face
of an angel. I love you very much x

Chapter One

Steam swirled in the air as Will Johnstone took the lid off the bone marrow broth that had sold like proverbial hotcakes since he'd insisted it went on the menu.

"Smells delicious," Stacey, the new waitress, said with a wink.

Will smiled weakly. She had been flirting with him ever since she'd started. He would have to get one of the waiters to fill the poor girl in. She didn't stand a chance.

To the untrained eye, the kitchen seemed to be in total pandemonium, but Will understood every move of this dance. He should. He'd been sous chef at Haven in Shoreditch for three years.

Serving under renowned chef, Anton Romano, he'd learnt all the foibles that his cantankerous boss preferred. As usual, Anton patrolled the pass where the plated meals waited to be served. If they stayed there longer than three minutes, he would scream at the restaurant staff until he went hoarse.

The month of August meant the traditional lull while valued customers enjoyed time on the beach in some far-flung place. Haven had that reassuringly expensive air that meant the clientele was more London's high society rather than tourists. Will had decided to use this time to test out new dishes before the inevitable surge in September that built steadily to Christmas.

"Are you going to let all the air get to that fucking broth?" Anton shouted across the room. Will realised Anton meant him and dropped the lid with a clatter.

He didn't even bother replying. Anton would be on to something else by now. That appeared to be the mousy new waitress whom he seemed determined to drive out of the door in less than two days. Will couldn't remember if that would be a personal best for Anton or not.

These days, he didn't even bother getting to know the wait staff unless Gustav, the maître d', tipped him off that they'd lasted the first month. They would tend to stay on then.

Will hated kitchens in August. The heat outside made it unbearable. He'd often tried to persuade Anton to reduce the number of hot dishes they served but Anton wouldn't have any of it. He didn't seem to feel the heat or the cold.

The intensity of the kitchen had started to lessen, the orders coming in slower. Anton stalked past him towards his office.

"Anton, could I have a —?" Will started.

"You may not," came the reply.

The staff regarded Will with amusement. They loved it when Anton treated him like shit. Anton liked to play a divide-and-rule game in his kitchen. He ruled with a culture where he positively encouraged climbing on top of colleagues, and at least three people were eyeing Will's position.

The smell of the duck main being prepped at the next station filled Will's nostrils. Anton might be a bastard, but he was an absolute genius too.

It had gone eleven and there would be no more orders. His body ached, but he had that adrenalin rush he loved after a mad shift. It would be hours before he could even think about sleep. As the staff scrubbed everything in sight, he made his way through to the office.

Anton sat with his feet up on the desk, engrossed in a recipe book that could have dated to Noah's time on the ark.

"That looks interesting," Will said. Ever the optimist, he could almost imagine one day the ice thawing, and Anton bothering about their working relationship.

Anton snapped the book shut with a bang and put it in his drawer. He scowled at Will, daring him to speak. Tonight clearly would not be that night.

As a concession to his seniority, Will had the honour of being able to hang his coat and bag up in Anton's office rather than the changing area. Instead of engaging with a riled Anton, he chose retreat.

He could visualise the cold bottle of Sancerre in the fridge at home if bloody Angela hadn't stolen it.

"This came for you," Anton said.

Putting his jacket on, Will turned around to see Anton holding up a letter. Will frowned. *Who sends letters these days?*

"It's from head office," Anton continued. His expression suggested he was passing something toxic to Will.

Head office was Anton's kryptonite. People only mentioned it if they absolutely had to. Anton had this fantasy that Haven was his own personal restaurant. He didn't want to accept that they were really being bankrolled by a Chinese investment firm. Most of the communications with head office were done by Will. It was nice to know he came in useful for the boring stuff.

"Weird they didn't just email," Will replied.

Anton stood and wandered to the drinks cupboard they had in the office, that Will had been warned on pain of death to never touch.

"Fancy a whisky before you go?" Anton said, trying to come across as friendly which really did not suit him.

Will could have been knocked down with a feather. "Erm…fine. Just a small one."

He poured a generous slug of Will's favourite, Hibiki. His mouth started to come alive in anticipation.

Anton raised his glass. "To Haven."

"Haven," Will replied.

He took a sip. His tastebuds exploded with all the different flavours of honey, orange, sandal and oak. They fought and danced together as he took a second to enjoy it.

"Good stuff," Anton said, smacking his lips.

"Amazing. My absolute favourite."

"A man of taste," Anton said, walking to his chair and sitting. He gestured to the chair in front of the desk.

Will lowered himself and waited. This Hibiki had more strings attached to it than a double bass.

"It seems one of the little shitcans out there has made a complaint," Anton said.

Everything slotted into place now. Anton didn't want to lose face in the kitchen but didn't mind trying to curry favour behind closed doors. *What a wily bastard.*

Anton pushed the bottle to his side of the desk. Will sank in his seat with a feeling of gloom coming over him. This was going to be a long session.

* * * *

An hour later and an exhausted Will let himself into his apartment, the remains of the bottle of whisky gurgling around in his backpack and his ears still ringing from Anton's rant.

Angela lay on the sofa with the TV blaring out a repeat of a soap opera. She opened her eyes as he put his bag down. "What time is it?" she said, stretching.

"Just gone two."

She frowned. "You're late."

"Ugh. Anton needed a friend."

"I thought he hated you."

Will stared out of the floor-to-ceiling windows at the view of Canary Wharf. He had to take three Tubes to get to work but he'd bought this place when he'd got his first professional job and wouldn't give it up for anything.

"One of the waitresses has made a complaint. I'm getting dragged into it. Lucky me."

Angela sat up and leant across to retrieve her half-drunk glass of wine. "And he wants you to defend his honour I suppose," she replied, taking a sip.

Will couldn't even be bothered to get a glass for himself, instead just holding his hand out. Angela gave him the glass, still staring at him.

"Got it in one." He took a sip. "Hey that's my bloody Sancerre."

Angela crawled across the velvet couch to his end and snuggled up to him.

"You're the best friend a girl could wish for."

"And you're a bloody thief."

"But you love me."

Will gently swatted her on the head. "Just as well, isn't it?"

Angela had been a waitress at Haven when he'd first started. It hadn't taken long until someone had seen her potential and she'd soon made a name for herself in the world of PR. He'd tried to get her to help the restaurant, but she despised Anton and refused to put her name to making him a success.

"It was only a matter of time before someone took that wanker on," she said, yawning.

He couldn't even argue. Anton played a dangerous game with his sexist comments. Will didn't know if he would cover Anton's arse yet again or gamble by telling the truth.

Whatever happened, it would have to wait for another time.

"How was your day?" he asked as he drained the glass. Sometimes he forgot about the world outside Haven.

"Oh, you know, went to the gym, had a few meetings, applied for a job in New York."

"Whoa, what?"

"Relax. I won't get it. They want someone to run a massive campaign for a baking show over there. Everyone is going for it. I've got no chance."

He thought about life without her. It didn't seem very appealing. He extracted himself from Angela and stood.

"I'm having a shower then bed. I'm knackered."

"You know, if you came out from behind those bloody cookers once in a while, bed might be a more exciting option."

Not this again. He walked over to his bedroom door. "Change the record before the morning, please. Good night."

As he closed the door, she shouted, "Your penis is begging to be released, William Johnstone."

He stripped down and threw his uniform in a heap in the corner, catching sight of himself in the mirror. At thirty-five years old, he still had his looks. The six-pack he'd crafted so diligently in his twenties might have disappeared, but he didn't brush up too badly.

He tried to remember the last time he'd had sex. *Ah yes. Brian.* The guy from the gym. He frowned—that had been his birthday treat to himself. His birthday was in April. It was now August.

Perhaps Angela had a point.

Another task for tomorrow then.

Chapter Two

It had been quite the twenty-four hours, and Hardeep Kaur's mother would be waiting not so patiently to get the lowdown.

She hadn't fancied the fete. The night before, she had been in charge of the catering for the curry night at the pub, The King's Arms. Cooking for fifty people had taken it out of her. Then when landlord, James Durkin, had announced his love for not one but two men, she had struggled to get a wink of sleep.

Hardeep chuckled to himself as he walked down Queen Street towards home. Usually there would be plenty of people to pass the time of day with, but the place was like a ghost town. Nothing much happened in Napthwaite so to have a gay throuple in their midst then the events of today, the place would need a bit of time to right itself.

He walked around the side of the post office he and his mother ran, shuddering at the thought of the endless customers tomorrow who would want to dissect everything. He would leave his mother to do that.

He ran up the stairs to the flat he shared with his family. Inside, the small kitchen still had pots and pans piled up, and in the lounge, his mother, Mohinder, sat in her chair by the window with her ever-present knitting. His teenage daughter, Satinder, lay on the sofa with the latest addition to the family, a one-year-old French bulldog named Beeb, snoozing on top of her.

None of them even acknowledged his presence. He would soon change that. "Oh hi, Hardeep. Have you eaten? Would you like to sit down?" he asked himself.

They ignored him, engrossed in the TV programme they were watching.

"Hardeep, you've worked hard putting the coconut shy away. Very good of you after Matthew got taken away in that ambulance."

Beeb leapt off Satinder as she spun around on the coach. Mohinder stopped mid-stitch and stared at him.

"I thought that might waken you up. Shift." He tapped his daughter's feet out of the way and sank onto the sofa.

Mohinder resumed her knitting.

"Tell us then," Satinder said eagerly. Clearly her thirst for information came from her grandmother.

"He will," Mohinder muttered. "Let him have his moment of glory."

He'd known she would be furious she'd missed all the action. "Jealous, Mother? You like to break the news around here."

Mohinder gave him an icy stare. "You can overbake a pudding, you know. Spit it out."

He had tortured them long enough.

"Fine, I'll talk. Poor old Matthew Johnstone just went down like a deadweight. In the middle of everyone. He'd been having a right slanging match with James. Well, not James as such—bloody Liz. One minute she's determined to run that teacher he's with out of town, the next she's defending him to the hilt. I can't keep up."

Mohinder seemed to be analysing this information. No doubt she would have a statement to make in good time.

"Napthwaite is getting exciting," Satinder said. "Three gay men in the pub and death at the fete."

Hardeep tapped her on the leg. "He's nowhere near dead. Don't say things like that, young lady."

Beeb jumped up on the sofa but came to him for a fuss. Of course he did. He naturally gravitated to the person who fed and walked him. Satinder had begged for a dog for months and had got bored with Beeb in days.

He scratched the little dog behind his ear, which he loved.

"Did they say what caused it?" Mohinder said at last.

"Not sure, but they got the defibs out, so must have been the heart."

Mohinder chewed her lip thoughtfully. "I guess that confirms he has one then."

"Mother. Don't you start. He's a neighbour of ours."

Mohinder put her knitting down and stared at him. "He's a nasty piece of work. Always has been. I don't wish ill on him, obviously."

He couldn't argue with her. Matthew Johnstone stalked around Napthwaite like he owned each brick and could pass judgement on every villager. He stood on all the committees, forcing his opinions on all and sundry.

"I thought he and Liz were in cahoots anyways," she said, lost in thought. "He didn't like that gay teacher being here any more than she did."

Beeb got up on Hardeep's lap and promptly fell asleep. He rubbed the dog's belly. "I for one hope he makes a recovery," he said.

"Mr bloody Perfect over there," Mohinder muttered to herself. "Bad things come in threes, so no doubt we'll need your good karma over the next few days."

Satinder frowned at Hardeep. "Threes? What else has happened?"

"Have you forgotten last night? Three gay men wandering around the village. All I can say is I'm glad you were born a girl, Satinder."

Satinder sat upright on the couch and glared at her grandmother. "That is a terrible thing to say, Granny. They have every right to live where they choose and how they choose."

Mohinder turned to Hardeep. "See? This is the crap she gets from that bloody phone she's glued to morning, noon and night."

He could feel yet another row brewing and put his hand on his daughter's foot.

"Mother, Satinder is fifteen and has opinions. I happen to agree with her as well."

Satinder smiled at him.

Mohinder let out a huff of indignation. "Of course, I'm in the wrong again."

"This time you are, Granny. It's the twenty-first century, and people don't think like you anymore. Thank goodness."

Mohinder threw her knitting down. "Don't worry, I will probably be dead like Matthew bloody Johnstone soon. Then you can have all the ideas you bloody like."

Mohinder could fly off the handle at a moment's notice, and her granddaughter generally matched her. This time was no exception.

"That's right. Make it all about you," Satinder snapped. "I'm saying that people can live how they like these days. They don't need you gossiping to your cronies about it either."

"Are you going to let her speak to me like that?" Mohinder said, glaring at him.

"Of course, I'm not. Satinder, apologise to your granny."

Satinder leapt up. "Sorry, Granny. I'm sorry that you can't find it in yourself to care about someone who has done a really brave thing."

Before Hardeep could interject any further, Satinder stormed out of the room. He shuddered as the kitchen door banged, disturbing the pile of pans which clattered to the floor. Beeb leapt up barking at the noise.

Mohinder was next on her feet. "This house is like a bloody lunatic asylum," she shouted. "I'm going for a lie down. And shut that bloody dog up." She, too, stormed across the room.

"Mum, wait. I'll give her a stern talking-to. I promise."

Mohinder turned and perched on the end of the sofa. "No, don't," she said. "Poor girl has had enough to contend with. She needs a mother. I wish I could fill that gap, but I can't."

She might be a force of nature, but he loved her with every fibre of his being. "You do us both proud. I would never have got through it without you."

Mohinder's face softened. "You're my boy. Whatever it takes, eh?"

"Whatever it takes," he replied.

"Although she's better off without that bloody harlot of a mother. She thinks she's some saint and I bite my tongue, Hardeep, I honestly do. If she knew it all, she'd soon change her tune."

Hardeep shuddered. "She'll never know what her mother is like. I'd rather she mourned a saint than lived with that witch. I'll go and talk to her."

Mohinder got up. "And if she thinks I'm not discussing the news of the day with my friends, she has another think coming. This is the biggest thing to happen to Napthwaite since the Queen's visit in 1998."

She winked at him as she went into her bedroom. Hardeep stroked Beeb slowly, calming him.

"The women in this house are crazy," he said to the dog. He placed him on the other side of the sofa and covered him with a blanket. "Right, I'd best go and sort one of them out."

He stepped over the pans festooned around the kitchen floor and let himself out through the back door. Satinder sat on the wall, staring up at the fells. His heart ached for her. He had grown up in Leeds and had had all the fun of the city when he had been her age. A village was a good place for kids, but it must feel like a prison to a teenager.

He sat with her.

"Don't start," she said, not even meeting his gaze.

"You shouldn't talk to her like that, you know. She loves you."

Satinder sighed. "I know. I'll tell her I'm sorry. I…"

Hardeep reached for her hand which she let him hold. "I know, love. We didn't do you any favours moving here."

Satinder's eyes filled with tears. "It's not that. I love it here really. I miss her, that's all."

He put his arm around her and she snuggled into him. "I can't be a mother to you and nor can Granny. You're going to have to try and be thankful for that."

The moment shattered like glass as Satinder leapt up. Her hands balled into fists, she glared at him. "And I'm supposed to just forget about my mother, am I? She will come for me one day, then you'll both be sorry."

Hardeep rubbed his eyes. "Not this again. It's been eight years, Sat. She isn't coming."

"Then I'll find her. I'll be an adult soon and there's nothing you can do to stop me."

She didn't wait for him to reply and stomped up the stairs to the flat, every footstep ringing like a church bell on the wooden staircase.

Hardeep exhaled.

"Not more drama," came a voice. "I'm not sure little old Napthwaite can take it."

Jenny Holdsworth stood on the corner. He got up and walked over to her. "Teenagers make drama every hour of every day. Add my mother into the mix and we have fireworks."

"Oh dear. How is Mohinder dealing with the aftermath?"

Hardeep shrugged. "As we know, my mother is the most liberal and accepting woman in West Yorkshire, so she has no problems at all."

They burst into laughter.

"She'll get used to it like everyone will," Jenny said. "I'm very proud of those boys and that leap of faith. I'll be seeing you."

"Yes, you know what? Me too. I'll see you, Jenny."

Queen Street led to the green where the pub stood. James, Ed and Arthur had been through hell in the last few months but had found a way to love. Hardeep admired that.

It took great strength. Strength he had never found.

Chapter Three

"Another day, another boiling-hot kitchen," Will said to Anton, who sat morosely at his desk.

The prep for that evening had gone really well, and he had half an hour to grab something to eat before service started.

"What?"

"It doesn't matter," Will muttered.

He reached into his jacket for his phone. The restaurant had a little seating area for staff, and he'd helped himself to a tomato tart they were serving as a starter. He wondered if he should have got Anton one but then remembered he had only declared ceasefire last night. Before that he'd been a true bastard. He could get his own bloody dinner.

Outside a couple of the staff were smoking. They made way for him as he came through and sat at the rickety old bistro table that Anton had gifted to the staff as though he were making all their wildest dreams come true.

Mid-August in London could either be soaking wet or lovely and warm. Luckily today was the latter. Half an hour to himself in the sunshine would be just what he needed. It beat watching Anton sulk in the office or getting bothered every ten seconds if he ate in the staff room.

He took a forkful of the tart. They had made it before and this time didn't disappoint. The pastry crumbled in the mouth but not on the fork and the acid of the cherry tomatoes cut through the cheese curd. This would sell out before the end of the day, no problem.

He made a mental note to praise Simon, the pastry chef. Once he'd realised that Anton didn't do encouragement, he'd made it a point to over do so with the staff. They loved him for it.

A pigeon leapt up on the wall and cooed. Will narrowed his eyes. "Oh, hello. Is there something I can help you with?"

The pigeon pointedly looked at the plate. Well, Will imagined that he did. Either way he broke off a bit of pastry and threw it. No doubt he would get shouted at for feeding vermin. He unlocked his phone and frowned. There were four missed calls from a number he didn't recognise. He never gave his number out and telesales people didn't usually try four times.

The answer machine icon also blinked.

Pressing one on the keypad, he put the phone to his ear.

"First new message. Received today at two-thirty-one."

Then a beep.

"Um, hello, this is a message for Will Johnstone. My name is Michael Fleming. I'm your father's gardener…"

This made Will sit upright. His father's gardener?

"Please could you contact me when you get this message? It's urgent."

Another beep.

"Next new message. Received today at three-fifty-three."

Beep.

"Will, this is Michael Fleming again. Please could you contact me as soon as you can?"

He terminated the call and sat stock-still for a second. Clearly it related to his father but what news would he be getting when he returned that call?

The yard lay deserted. Most of the staff liked to sit in the staff room, joking and messing about. He really didn't want to get bad news in front of Anton.

With a sigh he found the number on his missed calls list and pressed Dial.

"Hello?"

"This is Will Johnstone. I had a message to call you."

The long silence made him wonder if he'd pressed the right buttons. Kitchen equipment he could master in a morning, but smart phones weren't really his thing.

"Hello, Will. I'm sorry to have to tell you this, but your father has had a heart attack."

Cliched as it was, the world stopped for a second. Will took a moment to gather his thoughts. "How bad is it?"

"He's alive. They're keeping him in tonight with it being Sunday. The doctors will be round tomorrow to run tests. They asked me to tell you that it's probably a good idea if you come home."

"Fine, I'll make the arrangements. I…I don't have a key though."

"I have the key," Michael said. "I live at Bridge Cottage."

Bridge Cottage? Will remembered his old teacher used to live there. He used to sneak past the house when he and his pal David Chan got drunk in the churchyard.

"I'll be there as soon as I can."

Finishing the call, Will took a second to gather himself. He threw the tomato tart over the wall into the alley behind. The pigeon and his friends fell upon it, their excited cooing filling his ears as he walked inside the building. He ignored the staff and went straight into the office. Anton hadn't moved. *Probably counting down the hours until he can crack another bottle of expensive whisky open.*

"Anton."

He didn't even bother to react.

Will cleared his throat. "Anton."

"What is it?"

At thirty-five years old, he shouldn't be scared of asking for time off in an emergency, yet here he stood in front of Anton's desk like he'd been sent to the headmaster's office. "I have to go."

This caught his boss' attention. He frowned, the deep lines on his forehead becoming crevasses. "Go where?"

"My father has had a heart attack. I need to go to him."

Anton stared at him as though an alien species had crawled through the window and was asking him for his crème patisserie recipe. "Out of the question. We're fully booked tonight."

"Did you not hear me? My father has had a heart attack."

Anton pushed his chair from the desk. "I'm sorry to hear that, Will, but we have a full restaurant. What am I supposed to do?"

He absolutely would not lose his control, but the rage building up inside him made it a difficult mission. "You can cover my station. They don't need you breathing down their necks on the pass for one night."

An angry shade of red swept across Anton's already ruddy complexion. "And am I supposed to clean the floors after service?"

"No, the staff can do that. As usual."

Anton seemed almost lost for words for a second. "No, sorry. I need to do so much paperwork. You'll have to go tomorrow."

Will put his hands on the desk and leant forward. "You just reminded me. I have that interview with head office tomorrow. I'll have to call and rearrange. Or perhaps I'll do it over the phone. It's probably best to get it over with now. Don't want to delay their investigation."

Anton recoiled. For all the time he had worked here, Will had been no bother. He had obviously stunned his boss.

"Sounds a bit like blackmail to me," Anton managed.

Will wasn't in the mood to play cat and mouse. "Can I book a train for the morning or not?"

He had Anton cornered.

"Fine. How long do you want?"

He hadn't even considered this. "I've no idea until I get there. It might be a week, or it might be a month."

"A bloody month?"

Will allowed himself to sigh. "I have enough leave seeing as you never let me take any over summer."

Anton threw a pen down on the desk. "Try and make it in between. Is everything ready for tonight's service?"

Will tried to stop his jaw dropping. His plan seemed to be working. If he'd known Anton had been this easy to play, he would have done it years ago. "Yes."

"Go on then. Get out of my sight."

Will didn't hang around for him to change his mind. He grabbed his bag and walked straight out of the restaurant and set off home.

When he got there, he was confronted by Angela doing a keep fit routine in front of the TV. She leapt out of her skin as she turned mid star jump and saw him in the doorway.

"Jesus Christ, Will. You nearly gave me a heart attack."

From out of nowhere, Will burst into tears. Angela turned the TV off and guided him to the sofa.

"What on earth's the matter, babe?"

"It's my dad," he managed. "He's had a heart attack."

A sweating Angela sat next to him. "Go on," she said.

He told her about his call from Michael and subsequent blackmail of Anton.

"Serves the tight sod right. He gets more than his money's worth out of you."

"I don't know why I'm so worked up," Will said. "It's not like I'm close to my dad."

Angela rubbed his shoulder. "It doesn't matter. He's your dad. You're allowed to be upset."

Will couldn't let himself go to pieces. "Thanks. I think I need a shower then I'll have to pack a case." He stood.

"Have you eaten?"

He thought about the tomato tart that would be long gone by now and shook his head.

"Pizza it is then. I've done most of that workout, so I can afford to splurge."

After spending longer in the shower than usual, he managed to get himself together and packed. He had no idea what to take so threw as much in as his case would stand. When he went into the lounge, Angela had changed into her pyjamas and a bottle of wine sat open on the coffee table.

"I need to book a rail ticket. Or should I just leave it until I get to the station?" Will wondered.

Angela put her phone down on the arm of the sofa. "All done. I've just emailed you the confirmation. You can pick the tickets up at the station in the morning. You're getting the ten o'clock train, gets you into Leeds at just before one. I checked and you can get a bus from there."

He sank down next to her and kissed her on the cheek. "What would I do without you?"

"Pizza is on its way."

She filled their glasses and handed him one. He took a sip. It was good stuff.

"Is this the same Sancerre?"

"It is. I replaced it since you had a face on."

He took a sip and let the chilled white wine flood his system. The world had finally stopped. He had been on fast forward since getting the call from Michael. He had to let his emotions in sometime and now seemed like the perfect opportunity. "I bet he won't even be glad to see me."

"I can guarantee you he will, even if he doesn't say it."

She didn't know his father. To call him difficult was like saying Napoleon had anger issues. "I don't have the same relationship with my dad as most people do with theirs. I've told you."

"You've not told me much."

He sighed. "It's a cliché but he just sort of closed down when Mum died."

"You were twelve, right? What was she like?"

Even now, more than twenty years later, the lump in his throat appeared when he thought about his mother. "Yeah. The best mother in the world. She could knit, sew, sing, dance… My dad was totally different in those days. We would have days out and holidays. It was perfect."

She rubbed his leg. The best thing about Angela was that she knew when words were needed and when they weren't.

"Then one day, I came home from school and Mrs Turnbull was in the kitchen. Mum and Dad had been in Harrogate for the day, Christmas shopping. She stepped out in front of a bus and that was it. Gone."

Angela looked shocked. "I had no idea. I assumed she had been ill or something."

"Nope. Just one of those things. No one to blame. Dad blamed me though. Fuck knows why. He just changed. Don't get me wrong, he did his best for me. Money was always available."

The doorbell rang and Angela went to retrieve the food. She clattered about in the kitchen, getting things ready. Will tried to relax but the thought that he could be without his father too, no matter how distant they were, played over and over in his mind.

"Grub up," Angela declared.

He sat at the breakfast bar. The smell of the pizza cut through his lack of appetite, and his stomach let out a rumble of indignation at having been neglected so long.

"When did you last go up there?" Angela said, her mouth full of mozzarella and pepperoni.

He thought about it for a second. "Shit, it must be ten years. Dad had some boring garden party for the parish council and demanded I show up and demonstrate my skills. He didn't want to see me, just brag. I didn't last two days before I got the hell out of there, back to London."

"I think you're going to have to let up on him a bit," Angela said. "I know I don't know it all, but if he's weak, you can't start arguing the minute you get there."

"I know. We just rub each other up the wrong way. Our twice-yearly lunches at the V&A Café are about our limit."

Angela reached across the counter and squeezed his hand. "Your limits are going to have to be widened, my love."

The realisation of what he had to do started to set in. "I don't think I can do this, Ang."

"I don't think you have a choice, babe."

Chapter Four

Andrew Norris' cottage stood on the fells overlooking the village. He sat on the bench in the front garden, watching the sun climb in the sky, his black Labrador, Sally, at his feet.

Pots and pans crashed in the kitchen. Sally lifted her head, seemingly deciding if the situation required her input, but put it down again.

The head of Andrew's best friend, Lisa, appeared out of the kitchen window. "You have literally nothing of any use in this kitchen."

"I have a microwave and a tin opener. What more do I need?"

"I brought everything with me for a fry-up."

She disappeared into the kitchen where he could hear her rooting through his cupboards. Sally stood and stretched. She glanced at him, exuding disapproval at their little bubble being disturbed.

"I know, princess," he said, stroking her. "It won't last much longer. She'll be on her way to work soon."

A heron flew overhead. He watched the graceful way it glided through the sky. He'd seen them at Thorpe Tarn but never in the air.

His thoughts were disturbed by Lisa plonking herself down next to him. "I'm bringing all my own stuff next time." She raised a glass of orange juice. He reached to the floor and raised his.

"Cheers. Here's to mad fetes and gay love affairs."

They clinked glasses.

"You just missed a heron," he said.

Lisa made a face and swigged her drink. "All right, David Attenborough."

Andrew stuck out his tongue. He had met Lisa about a week after he'd moved to Napthwaite. She lived in the next village, Stockley Bridge, and ran a microbrewery. They had got chatting in her shop and bonded over a love of real ale.

They sat in silence, contemplating the day. Lisa was a dynamo but valued simple companionship too. If he had been that way inclined, he would have married her on the spot.

"On the way home, I'm calling in at The King's. James is probably shagged out and will easily agree to stocking my new ale."

The King's Arms. That hadn't been far from his thoughts in the last day or so. After the landlord, James Durkin, had declared his relationship with a farmer and a teacher, he supposed most of the village had been thinking about them.

"No wonder James didn't want to go for a drink with me. He had two on the go already."

Lisa put her arm through his and snuggled into his shoulder. "Your time will come."

Andrew snorted. "I doubt it. They're bloody crazy. One partner is enough for anyone. Two could kill you."

"You're too handsome to be this negative about love, you know," Lisa said, sitting up.

"I'm old and set in my ways. I only need Sal, don't I, girl?"

On cue, Sally sat up and put her head on his thigh. He stroked her.

"She's beautiful," Lisa said. "But she won't keep you up at night."

He had started to tire of this conversation. She meant well but even so, there was a line. "I like my sleep."

"Andrew. You're thirty-five years old. You need some excitement. I've started dating this guy from Harrogate. He's in marketing. I bet he knows loads of gay men. Why don't you let me set you up? We can make it a double date."

He hated being managed. "No thanks. I'm happy as I am."

"But…"

"Lisa, I said no thanks."

Hurt crossed over her face but she only had herself to blame.

"I love that you care," he said, taking her hand. "But I'm poison to men. I've accepted that and so should you."

"Bullshit," she barked. "I may have only known you for less than a year, but I can tell a decent guy when I see one. What happened?"

He got up from the bench. "I'd better get the knives and forks sorted."

She caught his arm before he started to move. "You can tell me, you know."

"I can't. Please leave it, Lis. I just can't."

To her credit, she did leave well alone, and they got back on an even keel over a feast of bacon, sausages and eggs. Sally couldn't contain her excitement. His usual cereal and microwave meal for one didn't result in this many treats.

"I'd best be going," Lisa said, glancing at her watch. "I've got twenty minutes to talk that man round before I have to be in the office. I'll leave you with the washing up as a special treat."

She kissed him on the cheek and set off out of the door. He took a last swig of coffee before feeling eyes on him. He jumped when Lisa had her head stuck through the window.

"I left that topic of conversation on a temporary basis, Andrew Norris. I'm watching you and I'm not going to let you waste your life."

Before he could reply, she had gone.

He threw a piece of bacon rind to a grateful Sally before clearing the dishes away. He didn't need anyone else.

His counsellor had told him he had built a sanctuary in Napthwaite and whilst understandable, it might not be the best thing. He needed to learn to let people in. He had done that with Lisa.

That would have to be enough for the time being.

He went to make another coffee and opened the fridge, which lay empty as usual.

"We'd best get supplies, girl." Andrew picked up her lead, and Sally stood obediently in front of him while he clipped it to her collar. The trust in her eyes made his heart swell. He kissed her on the top of the head. "You're my number one and that's that."

They set off down the lane towards the village. Sally liked to stop endlessly to have a sniff and he didn't have the heart to hurry her, so they proceeded slowly.

As they reached the green, the last few remnants from the fete were being tidied away.

He saw James, Arthur and Ed walking towards Queen Street, and hung back. The last thing he wanted was to get into conversation with them. Nothing had happened between him and James, but he felt awkward anyway.

They went down the alley behind Poole's shop. *Interesting.* They must be going to James' sister, Liz's house. That was a turn up for the books. It hadn't been a week since she had been trying to drive Arthur out of the village.

He sat on the bench opposite the church to fiddle with Sally's lead that had got caught in her collar. Hardeep, the postman, came and sat on the other side of the bench. He had a French bulldog with him, who showed a great deal of interest in Sally.

"I didn't know you had a dog," Andrew said.

Hardeep sighed. "Sat begged until I gave in. Now I'm the sucker who goes for walks twice a bloody day."

"Kids, eh? What's he called?"

Hardeep shifted, embarrassed. "Beeb. Short for Bieber as in Justin. Imagine how stupid I look shouting him at night."

Andrew stroked Sally. She had already been named when he'd picked her up from the dogs' home, and he thanked his lucky stars her previous owner had been sensible about it.

"Quite the day yesterday," Andrew said.

"I'll say. Apparently, Matthew rallied overnight and is home. I can't keep up."

Andrew frowned. Matthew had looked in a bad way the day before. "Is that wise?"

"I heard that he'd checked himself out, but you know Mrs Turnbull. She likes to add a bit of flair to her stories."

He remembered his light-hearted grilling at the hands of Mrs Turnbull when he'd arrived in the village. She didn't like anything happening without her knowledge. "I bet she's had the best weekend of her life."

Hardeep glanced at him before sniggering. "She's round our house for morning coffee as we speak. On a Sunday. My mother lapped it up."

"Did you have to get out?"

Andrew glanced at Hardeep. They had exchanged pleasantries before when he'd delivered parcels, but this could be the first proper conversation they'd had. Hardeep was a handsome guy with thick dark hair and the start of stubble. The razor must have the day off on a Sunday. It suited him too.

Absentmindedly Andrew stroked his own blond beard. He'd grown both his hair and his beard when he came here. He loved it.

"When Kathleen Brockbank from the newsagents turns up, that's my cue to leave. They can go for hours raking over the news of the day."

"Sounds like you're outnumbered."

Hardeep considered it for a second. "I guess I am. I always have been. Even when I was married."

His face changed, and he bent down to extract Beep from sniffing some old burger that had been discarded the day before.

Andrew wouldn't pry. He hated that. If people wanted to give him information, they would do so under their own steam. "Has anyone heard from Matthew's son?" he asked.

Hardeep glanced down the road, where the gates of Thorpe Hall could be seen past the bridge.

"I spoke to that gardener of Matthew's last night when I took this one out. He's spoken to him and he's supposed to be coming up. He needed to sort things out with work. He works in a restaurant in London."

The gardener had to be one of the most handsome men Andrew had ever set eyes on when he'd appeared at the fete to go with Matthew to the hospital. "That gardener. I wouldn't get anything done if he was toiling away in my front beds."

Hardeep shifted a little uncomfortably.

"Sorry," Andrew said with a wink.

Hardeep got up. "Well, I'd best be getting home. I promised Satinder I'd run her to Leeds."

"She's a lucky girl. Most fathers would make her get the bus."

Hardeep had a lopsided smile and his eyes really lit up. "I chose to live here, not her. I've got to play fair."

They wandered towards Queen Street. Sally had decided the young Beep required her care and made sure he kept up. They arrived at Poole's, which lay in darkness.

"Since when have they closed on a Sunday?"

"It's Liz's birthday so she's having a family party."

Andrew groaned. "Come on, Sal. Holton it is. Ugh, I hate supermarkets on a Sunday. Well, I'll be seeing you, Hardeep."

"Yeah, see you, Andrew."

He started to turn towards home before stopping. "I've had an idea. Do you fancy taking these two for a walk sometime?"

Hardeep's face lit up. "I'd love it."

Andrew got his phone out to take Hardeep's number. At that moment a taxi appeared coming past the village hall and drove down the road towards them. In the back sat an incredibly good-looking man.

"That must be the son," Hardeep said. "I will go and drop that info to the three witches in my house. My mother hates it when I get news before she does. Life's simple pleasures, eh?"

"Thorpe Hall definitely attracts handsome men."

They swapped numbers and Andrew set off. As he walked across the green, he glanced down the road to the hall.

That guy in the cab had been dazzling. Andrew might not want to share his heart, but he could be persuaded to share his bed with a handsome stranger passing through. That would definitely be permissible.

Chapter Five

Will felt like the Prodigal Son as the taxi drew up to the looming Victorian house. To call it a mansion would be generous. But with its seven bedrooms and large downstairs rooms, it wasn't a mere house. It had originally been the manor. Some might say his father still saw it as that.

His father.

Anxiety coursed through his veins at the very thought. Visiting him on home turf gave the disadvantage to Will. He got his case out of the car and proceeded to the big oak door. How many times had he banged it after a particularly intense row with Matthew?

Today an incredibly handsome man stood on the step. He held his hand out, and Will noticed it was covered in soil.

"Michael Fleming. You must be Will."

Will shook his hand. A strong, manly handshake. "Pleased to meet you."

Michael glanced up at Matthew's bedroom window. "He came home this morning."

Will frowned. "He came home? But I thought it was serious."

"It is but he insisted."

Matthew Johnstone clearly hadn't changed. He knew what was best for everyone and everything. Of course, a doctor's advice wouldn't stop him from doing what he wanted.

"Is he alone?"

Michael nodded.

"I'd best go in then."

"He's not in the best of moods. I've offered to go into Holton to get some things."

This man made him feel quite inferior. Not only did he have the most engaging eyes Will had ever seen but he actually came across as a decent person.

"It's Sunday—you must have plenty of things at home. Don't worry about it. I'll take it from here."

Michael's face lit up with a grin. "You sure about that?"

The big question. He didn't feel particularly sure. "Yes, but do keep checking on me. I have a feeling I might need back up."

Michael winked. "Got it. I'll be weeding the Perlita bed tomorrow. Just over there." He pointed to a glorious flowerbed in the corner. It was filled with blooms of pinks and whites. The name caught in Will's throat. Matthew had named the bed after his mother.

"Has he given all the beds names?"

The gardener blushed. "That was my idea. It made it easier for us to talk about them when we were planning the overhaul of the garden."

Matthew had been very excited by the new gardener when he'd arrived in the spring. He had told Will all about it. They'd both been thankful it had taken most of the dutiful lunch they had shared in May.

"What's that one then?" Will said, pointing to one mirroring the bed named after his mother.

"Ah, that's the Churchill bed."

Will snorted. "I don't think I want to know any more." He picked up his case and made his way towards the house.

"The Will bed is in front of the lawn round the other side. If you were interested," Michael called after him.

The tears threatened to overwhelm him. He hadn't expected one named after him. "Thanks," he said, not turning to reveal his face. "I'll check it out later. I'd best see Dad. Can't put it off any longer." He pushed the heavy door open and a low bark sounded out around the old house. Suddenly a mound of fur appeared from nowhere and leapt up at him, nearly pushing him over.

"That's Titus," Michael said. "He's a darling."

The alsatian had his paws on Will's chest and eyes full of expectation for love. Will made a fuss of him. "I've heard all about you, boy. What a beautiful man you are."

The dog lapped up the attention before begrudgingly making way for Will to come in. He waved at Michael as he closed the door.

A handsome gardener and beautiful dog were a decent welcoming committee, but up the stairs, the main event waited for him.

He looked around the hallway. Not a lot had changed. His father had swapped the beige carpets for blue, but the pictures and ornaments were the same.

Spoils from his father's early years working in the Philippines.

"Michael, is that you?"

It was now or never. Feeling about ten years old, he climbed the stairs to the landing. Down to his left sat his childhood room. That would have to wait. Instead, he turned right and walked to the door at the end of the corridor.

The door he'd heard his father cry behind all those years ago. Gently he turned the handle and went in.

His father seemed to have aged twenty years since he'd last seen him. He lay propped up by pillows in the big bed. Will was taken aback at how pale and fragile he looked. The curtains were still drawn, letting in just a chink of light.

A small lamp lit the room but even so, Will had to peer to make sure it actually was his father. He always presented himself so smartly, so to see him with his hair mussed up, a day's growth on his face and creased pyjamas, came as a shock to Will.

Matthew squinted in the gloom. "Will? Is that you?"

Will tried to look cheerful as he walked into the room. "What's been going on, Dad?"

Matthew tried his best to look haughty, an impossible mission, but Will had to admire him for trying. "Pah, a load of fuss over nothing. I had a turn at the fete. Who the hell rang you?"

He hadn't expected a hero's welcome, but a smile might have been nice. Titus pushed the ajar door fully open and leapt up on the bed next to his master. This time Matthew's face did light up.

"Here he is. Looking after Daddy."

He stroked the dog, who settled down next to him, letting out a sigh before resting his head on the pillow.

Will strode over to the window and opened the curtains, letting the sunny August day in.

Matthew squinted. "Bloody hell, give a man some warning."

Approaching the bed, Will could see his father's weakness for himself. He had lost weight since Will had last seen him, and his hand shook as he reached for a glass of water that had been left on the bedstand.

"Can I get you anything?" Will asked.

"You can answer my question."

"Michael rang me. They were worried —"

Matthew dropped the glass, spilling the remains of the water over his chest. "Bugger it," he exclaimed.

Will leapt forward, grabbing a shirt that had been hung on the vanity stand next to the bed and started to mop the water up.

"I could have done that," Matthew grumbled. "I suppose you've come to make sure your inheritance is intact."

His ability to try for an argument hadn't been diminished. Will had to give him credit for that. "Nothing of the sort. I came to see if you're all right."

"I'm fine. I told you, I just had a turn."

Will perched on the end of the bed. "Dad, you had a heart attack. Why on earth did you leave the hospital?"

Will's eyes were drawn to two photos in frames on the bedstand, one of his mother at her most beautiful and another of him as a little boy with Matthew. He remembered the day well. They had gone on holiday to Corfu and his father had challenged him to a sandcastle competition. Will had won and been so proud.

He focused on the two beaming faces, staring at his mother who had taken the picture. How could all that go in the blink of an eye?

"I'm not dying in one of those places."

"I thought you said it was just a funny turn."

Matthew seemed about to argue but stopped. "Caught out. I must be ill."

Will suddenly realised the responsibility he had taken on with no thought. If his father insisted on being at home, he would have to assume the responsible adult role. "And you did that without knowing I'd be here? Why on earth?"

"Bessie Turnbull said she'd call in to make me lunch, and Michael said he'd keep an eye on things."

Guilt started to enclose around Will's heart. In the last ten years his father had grown old, and he'd been so caught up in his life in London that he hadn't noticed.

"No need for that now. You have a top-class chef at your disposal."

"Won't they need you at work?"

Will would not let himself be goaded into an argument. "No, I've taken some leave. We'll see how things go. I thought I'd get you on your feet again, help you sort things out."

Matthew frowned. "Sort what things out?"

Will looked around the room. "This place for one. Maybe it's time to let it go. You have plenty of places in the village to choose from."

The bed shook as Matthew slammed his hand down on the duvet. Titus leapt off the bed and searched around for the source of the sudden disturbance.

"How dare you think you can come here and start saying things like that? Give this place up? It has been in our family for four generations."

"But—"

"I realise you won't be providing an heir, but is it acceptable to you that I spend out what is left of my life here before you try to get your hands on the money?"

"Dad…"

"Get out of my sight."

Will could see his father getting worked up. He didn't want to cause a relapse, so he got up and walked over to the door. He turned. His father had watched his every step. "I'll take the dog out, if you like. Maybe I can make myself useful there. Is there anything I can get you on my way back?"

Matthew turned his head on the pillow, staring out of the window. "Thank you, no."

"I came here to care for you, Dad. That's all."

Matthew didn't answer.

Will shut the door gently behind him. Titus, his new best friend, had come out with him. At least one resident of the house wanted him here.

He went downstairs and retrieved his case before heading up the stairs. This time he turned left and found himself in his bedroom. All traces of him had been removed except for a wooden car he had made at secondary school for his father. That sat on the windowsill. To his amazement, all his books from his childhood were still on a shelf underneath.

He raced over and took in the titles as though they were old friends. There were Famous Five adventures, the Narnia books and his all-time favourite, *The Hobbit*. He sat on the window seat and thumbed through the copy.

This had been a good friend to him when no one had understood him. The view out of the window was so familiar, the village in the distance surrounded by the hills that had been his jailors as a teenager.

From what he had seen when the taxi had brought him down Queen Street, nothing had changed. Well except for the two handsome guys who had stared into the car. Not counting his father, he'd seen three residents of Napthwaite and each of them had been gorgeous. Maybe things *had* changed a bit since his last visit. *Next thing, Mrs Turnbull will have had Botox and a breast lift.*

He chuckled to himself as he replaced the book on the shelf. Whether he liked it or not, he would be staying here for a while. He might as well explore his old stomping ground that he'd loathed for the best part of thirty years.

Before starting his trip down Memory Lane, he snuck his head around his father's bedroom door. Matthew lay fast asleep. Will watched him breathing from the doorway. He hoped being here would help his father rather than hinder him.

Letting the door close gently, he took a tour of the house. Most of the rooms were exactly as he remembered them. Some things had been replaced. His father had bought a huge TV screen for the cricket. It didn't really work next to the furniture his mother had filled the house with when they'd returned from the Philippines.

Once in the hallway, Titus sat patiently by the front door. Will could take a hint and grabbed the lead from the hook.

"Come on then, lad. Let's see what we can find out there."

They set off towards the village. Will thought his head might explode with all the memories that bamboozled his brain.

They walked over the bridge and onto the green, where Titus started to bark as a beautiful black Labrador came over to them.

Titus soon stopped his noise and the dogs got on with the business of having a good old sniff of each other. Will glanced up and recognised one of the men who he had seen when he arrived.

"Hello there," he said, walking over.

"Hi," Will said.

The man had blond hair scraped up into a bun and skin so deeply tanned that he had to work in the outdoors. "Andrew Norris and Sally's the dog," he said, holding his hand out.

"Will Johnstone," Will replied, shaking it.

"I figured as much."

Good old Napthwaite. Of course, his arrival would have been spoken about already. He half-expected Mrs Turnbull to appear from behind one of the trees that lined the street overlooking the green.

"How is your father?" Andrew continued.

Will sighed. "Sicker than he'd admit. I'm just off to find something decent to feed him tonight."

Andrew glanced up at Queen Street. "Poole's is closed, I'm afraid. Some family do."

"Poole's? That was Mr Brannigan's in my day."

"It's run by Liz Poole now. She manages to fill it with everything you don't want."

They laughed. "Liz Poole? Not Liz Durkin?"

Andrew shrugged his shoulders. "I've only been here a year, but it sounds right. Her brother, James, runs The King's."

James Durkin had been a couple of years below him at school and Liz two above. He remembered begging

James to let him play with him and Ed in the woods, but they wouldn't, calling him too young and too posh.

"I'd best see if the pub can do a takeaway, then."

"I can recommend the steak and ale pie. It's the best of a bad job in there. I had intended to get supplies myself but took the easy way out."

Sally and Titus were settled next to each other as if they were old friends.

"He's a beautiful dog," Andrew said.

"Yes. We've only just met, but I think we're going to be friends. Right, I'd best be getting on. See if I can find something to feed my dad with."

"Good luck with that. They're not known for their food."

Will gently tugged at the lead to let Titus know they were on the move. "I'm sure I can find something. Then I'll be Liz's best customer tomorrow. My father's cupboards are pretty empty."

"If you're at a loose end, a friend of mine is meeting me for a dog walk soon. I'm sure there's room for one more," Andrew said.

Will thought to himself. Did he want to make arrangements? He had no idea how long he would be here. It would be just like his father to banish him by nightfall.

"Why not?" he said. "Let's swap numbers. I'd best get Dad settled but next weekend?"

"Sounds like a plan."

They exchanged their details and Andrew set off up the road past the school. Will watched him from the pub doorway.

A date with a hot guy and hopefully his hotter friend. Angela would be very impressed.

Chapter Six

His father had turned his nose up at the congealed vegetable curry he had brought from the pub the night before, and Will could hardly blame him.

He toasted him the last of the bread and shuddered when he saw the butter he had to put on it. Things would have to change around here, whether his father liked it or not.

Putting the tray down on the bed, he walked over to the window and drew the curtains.

"You're obsessed with bloody light," Matthew grumbled.

Will ignored him. Titus lay on his usual spot on the bed, and Will stroked him behind the ear as he straightened the bedsheets.

"I could get a nurse you know," Matthew continued. "I don't need your help."

"No, Dad. Of course you don't. But you've got it and that's how it is for the time being."

Matthew sighed and tried to get himself comfy on the pillow, but his arms seemed too weak.

"Come here." Will took hold of him under his arms and effortlessly pulled him up in the bed. His father had never been a big man, but he hardly weighed a thing. "I'm going to build you up, whether you like it or not."

"I suppose all that money I spent putting you through university may as well be put to good use. So much for having your own place at thirty."

If Will remembered it correctly, that had been an ambition forced upon him by Matthew. He thought it best not to point this out. "Anything you need from the shop?"

Matthew made a face. "If I need anything in this world, Liz Poole won't be providing it."

Will went over and opened a window to get some fresh air into the stuffy room. "Perhaps we'll take a turn around the garden later? Get some fresh air."

Matthew nibbled on a piece of toast. A hopeful Titus was rewarded with a bit of crust. "Yes, you can see what Michael has been doing. He exhibited at Chelsea, you know."

Chelsea? At least his father still had plenty of cash to splash around. That would make him happy. "Titus," Will said.

The dog leapt off the bed at his call. Matthew raised his eyes. "Well, he likes you, that's for sure."

Will retreated as quickly as possible, glad to leave things on a positive note. He got his things together and, once again, he and Titus made their way into the village. They wandered up past the green.

"William Johnstone. There's a face I've not seen in a while." Mrs Turnbull stood in her front garden. She beamed across at him.

"Hello, Mrs Turnbull. Looking as beautiful as ever."

She giggled like a schoolgirl and fiddled with her hair. "I had a rinse put on for the fete. That's probably what you mean."

Her front garden had always been a riot of colour. She and her husband had loved being a talking point for anyone passing by.

"How is Mr Turnbull?"

Her face dropped. "Oh, he passed away a good few years ago. It's just me now."

"I'm sorry to hear that." He walked forward so only her garden wall separated them.

"How is your father? He scared us all."

Will knew how things worked. His father dropping down at the fete would be the biggest news to hit Napthwaite for quite a while. Mrs Turnbull would see it as her duty to get the latest updates.

"He's home, although I'm not sure it's a good idea. I've a telephone consultation with his doctor later."

She nodded sagely. "So you're here for a while then?"

Her interrogation technique had always been forthright. "For a while. Let's see how things go."

"I promised to get your father some shopping but no doubt you have everything under control."

"Yes, I'm just off to Brannigan's...er...Poole's for some things."

Mrs Turnbull raised her eyebrow as she absentmindedly deadheaded a rose. "You're very forgiving, I must say. I'm not sure I'd be putting money in her till."

Will frowned. "What do you mean?"

"You haven't heard?"

The game of cat and mouse bored him. "You're the first person I've spoken to. Perhaps you'd better fill me in."

Mrs Turnbull ushered him inside the house. Titus flopped down on the rug in front of the seat that she almost pushed him into. In a jiffy, she returned with two mugs of coffee and a chillingly eager expression on her face. "You remember James Durkin and Ed Cropper?"

He nodded.

"Turns out they've been having an affair. Right under our noses. I couldn't believe it."

James and Ed? They'd always been close at school. "Good luck to them then," he said, sipping his coffee.

"That's not everything," Mrs Turnbull continued. "A few weeks ago, a new person came to the school. Took up with Ed. Liz didn't like a queer...sorry, gay man teaching her son. A right hullabaloo started and ended with James declaring his love for both of them. In the pub on Friday night."

She sat back to let this piece of news sink in. *Napthwaite definitely has changed.*

"But what has that got to do with my father?"

Mrs Turnbull's face clouded over. "Your father...well, he agreed with Liz. They had quite a campaign going but when she realised her brother was caught up in it, everything changed. I guess blood is thicker than water. She turned on a sixpence and had a huge argument with your father at the fete when he said something to James."

Will could just imagine what his father had said.

"She got quite nasty, bringing up all sorts of things. Then he just hit the floor."

"I thought he had just collapsed? I didn't realise he had been arguing."

"Of course you didn't. No mind. You're here now. I'm sure your father appreciates that, no matter what went on."

Unease ran down his spine like molten lava. "Just what exactly did happen, Mrs Turnbull?"

She shifted in her seat. "I'm not sure it's my place to say."

"I think it probably is."

She smiled weakly. "She brought up that incident. You know. Before you went to boarding school."

Will closed his eyes. Of course she had thrown that at his father. He carefully placed his china cup on its saucer. "I think I'd best be going. Thank you for the update." He couldn't wait to get out onto the street and fill his lungs with some fresh air. The cloying scent of lavender in Mrs Turnbull's house mixed with her beady eyes scanning for any reaction had made him feel lightheaded.

Once he'd got himself together, he set off up towards Queen Street. There might be a more cosmopolitan crowd in this village these days, but the same stink of judgement permeated every square metre.

After tying Titus up outside, he stalked into the shop. A couple of villagers he didn't recognise were searching around the aisles in vain for something decent to eat. The stock could be mistaken for the same stuff that had filled the shelves the last time he'd been in here a decade ago. The inside had changed with garish shelving, and faded advertisements for tinned meat and custard powder lined the little wall space left. He remembered a lovely shop with sweets by the pound and Mr Brannigan, who would always give him a little extra.

He recognised Liz Poole immediately. She had been a knockout at school. Time had not been kind. Her greasy hair scraped back in an unflattering ponytail and the nylon tabard aged her. "Liz Durkin."

Recognition spread across her face. "Will Johnstone. It must be ten years."

"Something like that."

"How is your father?"

She had a nerve, he would give her that. "Why? Guilty conscience, Liz?"

Her face set into a hard stare. "I see you've been speaking to someone."

Folding his arms, he stared her out. "You always were a mouthy cow at school, and from what I've heard nothing has changed."

"That's right, it's all my fault."

"Are you going to deny it?"

She huffed and fiddled with some tins that had past their sell-by date stickers on. "You have no idea what's been going on."

"I know enough. Why did you have to drag me into it?"

This time she had the decency to look embarrassed. "I honestly don't know. My mouth just ran away with itself. Will, I'm sorry."

He glanced around the shop. The two customers had stopped what they were doing and were watching events unfurl. "I guess that's the best I can hope for from the likes of you. I can see there's nothing for me in here. I want to improve my father's health, not finish him off."

He made his way to the door. "Upset my father again and you'll have me to deal with."

* * * *

The rest of the week passed by with not much interest. Matthew and Will settled into a routine of sorts. Matthew had resolutely refused to leave his room, so Will had the house to himself. He'd spent most of the time taking stock in the kitchen. His father enjoyed cooking and had bought all sorts of contraptions. Once Will had got the bus to Holton and stocked up on quality food from the supermarket, he set to making some decent dishes.

What had shocked him had been his father's praise. That had never been forthcoming before but he seemed to be genuinely enjoying Will's creations.

On Friday night, the sunset lit up the sky with pinks. The birds were singing at top pitch and bees still buzzed around, putting in a late shift. He had come here to make changes and he had every intention of doing that.

He marched into his father's bedroom and retrieved the dressing gown from the back of the door. It could have been his imagination, but he could swear some colour had returned to Matthew's cheeks. Sitting up reading a biography on Nero, he put it down and removed his glasses.

"What do we have here?"

"No excuses. Let's get you into that garden."

Matthew sighed. "I'm fine where I am."

"You've been in here for nearly a week now. If you're that ill, you should be in hospital."

Will held the dressing gown up. For a split second he thought he'd lost the battle, but to his amazement, Matthew pulled the covers away.

"Fine. You win."

He got out of bed, but his legs seemed to wobble. Will dashed across and grabbed him by the arm. Matthew wrestled himself free and took the dressing gown. Putting it on himself, he looked at Will. "Lead on."

They walked downstairs and out into the garden. Matthew had put his wellies on at the kitchen door and with his pyjama bottoms billowing over the tops, made quite the image.

Once out, Matthew adopted the air of an inspector. He glanced at the shrubs and flowerbeds. "Michael has been keeping on top of things. That's something, I suppose."

"I'm sure you're paying him enough," Will replied.

They proceeded down the path. The air was still, and the sun still gave a warm glow when they walked in its light.

"It's looking wonderful," Will said.

The formal garden opened up to a long lawn that ran down to the boundary wall. New flowerbeds that had all sorts of blooms in them lined this wall.

"Which is the Will bed?"

Matthew stared at him. "The what?"

"Michael said you'd named one for me."

A flush spread across his father's neck. "The *William* bed is over there."

Will followed his gaze to a bed in the corner. In the middle sat his old racing car that he used to tear up and down the garden paths in as a child. Someone had given it a new paint job, but it still had the blue stripe on white. All the blooms that surrounded it were either blue or white. It was perfect.

"Dad, it's wonderful." He turned to his father. They held gazes for a second and Will could have basked in it for the rest of his life. But normality returned and Matthew started to rummage around in the flowers at their feet.

"You don't want to be stuck up here with me all the time. Maybe you could ask that girl you live with to come?"

A warning flag raised. His father had been determined that Will would fall in love with Angela and all "*that silly gay business*" would be a distant memory. "Maybe. I'm going on a walk tomorrow."

Matthew looked up. "Who with?"

"I got talking to a guy in the village. He's called Andrew."

"Ah yes, the forestry man. Yes, he's a wonderful chap. We had quite the conversation about dry rot."

"And Hardeep. The postman?"

Still a pleased smile remained on his father's face. The crisis seemed to be averted. "Hardeep is great. Has a daughter and cares for his mother."

Will could be fifteen all over again, asking his father's permission to go out. "I'm glad you approve."

"As long as it isn't James Durkin, Ed Cropper or that new teacher. This village has had enough to talk about in the last week. They don't need anything more."

They started to make their way to the house. "No fear of that, Dad. I have no intention of being talked about again."

Chapter Seven

Saturday morning dawned. Will had got up early and seen to Matthew's breakfast. Titus lay sprawled on the bed. "Laze around while you can, Titus," Will said to him. "I'm taking you on a big one today."

Matthew handed him the glass of water he'd taken his tablets with. "Ah yes the dog walk. Have a good time."

"Will you be all right?"

Matthew shifted uncomfortably. "Yes, Bessie Turnbull is calling in at lunch time."

Will stood with his hands on his hips. "And when did you arrange this?"

"She texted me last night. What of it?"

"If I find any trace of baking in this house, there will be trouble."

Matthew seemed to rev himself up to launch into a tirade before he caught himself. "If I wanted to eat baked goods, I would eat baked goods. I certainly would not hide evidence in my own home."

He picked up *The Telegraph* that Will had brought upstairs with him and gave it a stern shake to communicate that this conversation was at an end.

Beaten fair and square, Will left. He had no intention of fretting over an argument while out on this walk. He'd been looking forward to it all week. At the top of the stairs, he whistled, and a huge thud rang through the house before the alsatian appeared at the door.

"Come on."

Titus didn't need telling twice and bounded after Will, who put the lead on him then picked up his rucksack. Andrew hadn't mentioned lunch, but he liked to be prepared. Rainclouds threatened, but the forecast said it would be fine. *Typical Yorkshire.* Will checked his pack for the poncho he'd found in Matthew's coat cupboard.

He glanced at his watch. He'd agreed to meet Hardeep on the green at ten and it was quarter to now. About thirty seconds later, he found himself on the green with fifteen minutes to kill. Perching on the bench, he stroked Titus. A figure approached him, and Will squinted in the sunlight.

"Will Johnstone. I heard you were back."

"Hi, James. How have you been?"

"I'm sure you've heard how I've been," James replied. "Come into the pub one night. I'll buy you a drink."

"I'll do that."

James went into The King's Arms. Will couldn't get used to seeing these people from his past. Sitting on the bench, he marvelled at how quiet things were here. He couldn't remember the last time he had experienced proper stillness. The sun peeked out from behind the clouds, and he let himself enjoy the feeling of the warmth.

"Are you auditioning for a shampoo advert?"

He opened his eyes to one of the most handsome men he'd seen in a long time, including Andrew and Michael. Will could have lost himself in the man's dark brown eyes plus he had that whole gelled quiff and stubble thing going on. A sure-fire winning combination for Will.

"Sorry?"

"Just kidding you. Will?"

"Hardeep?"

They shook hands. Will glanced down at the man's big hairy forearms and pictured himself gripping them.

"You okay?" Hardeep said.

"Yeah sorry. Was miles away for a second."

"Anywhere nice?"

"Oh, I reckon so." Will stood, anxious to get moving and this embarrassing introduction behind them.

Titus looked down disdainfully at Beeb who valiantly tried to sniff him but lacked the height to achieve the task.

"They say dogs take after their owners. He is dangerously like my father at the moment."

They both laughed and the ice was broken. They set off up the road to Andrew's cottage. The two dogs took one side each of the two men.

"How are you finding being back?"

"It's not as bad as I thought it was going to be."

"What did you think we were going to do? Burn you on the green?"

They ambled along the lane, chatting until they reached Andrew's gate. He stood leaning on it with Sally waiting patiently at his feet. The sun glinted in his blond hair that he'd swept up in a bun. The tight-fitting T-shirt seemed to be struggling to contain his muscular build. Will found himself licking his lips. Andrew grinned as they approached.

Will thanked his lucky stars to be spending the day with a bit of eye candy. Being stuck in the house for a week and in a kitchen for what seemed like an eternity, it had been a while since he'd just hung out.

"Morning, gents," Andrew said when they got near.

Sally got in between Titus and Beeb, and before long the three of them were playing happily.

"They refused to speak all the way up," Will said with a grin.

"My Sally, the peacemaker."

"Where are we off to?" Hardeep asked eagerly.

Andrew pointed up the lane that went past his house. "I thought we'd go over the tops, follow the path down to Curlew Brow, then I can show you what we've been doing in work."

Will didn't really mind. He just loved being in the outdoors, taking in air that wasn't taxi fumes. They set off and fell into a rhythm. Will walked in the middle of the two tall men and at five-seven, he could empathise with poor Beeb trying keep up with the two bigger dogs.

"How is it going up there?" Hardeep asked.

"Really well," Andrew answered. "We should be done in a year or so, then in a good few hundred years, these hills will be lined by forests again."

Will frowned. He had only ever known these hillsides to be used for agriculture. "Won't that cut the village off?"

"Not a bit. It will shelter it, plus there won't be floods in the winter with all the root networks sucking the water up."

Napthwaite had always been prone to flooding. They had regularly had days off school because the power had gone down. Will usually had his friends over to the Hall where they would tear around, playing army in the garden.

Will was shocked to find himself out of breath when they got to the top of the hill. His fitness was long gone. He and Titus would have to deal with that during his stay here. The other two were barely panting.

"Come on, city boy," Andrew said, clapping him on the shoulder.

Will marvelled at how the man's hand encased his whole shoulder. His thoughts strayed to how those big hands would feel exploring every part of his body. He tried to banish the thought. Angela had been right in the fact he hadn't slept with anyone for a few months, but since taking a break from the kitchen, he had a one-track mind.

"How long are you here for?" Hardeep asked him.

"I'm not sure," Will replied. "Dad is doing well, but I don't really want to leave him just yet."

Andrew threw a stick and they watched as all three dogs ran for it. "Your work must be very understanding," he said.

"You're joking. My boss is a bastard. But he's got a HR investigation hanging over him, so he's open to me taking as long as I want."

"Blackmail? I like it," Hardeep said.

"We'll have to watch you," Andrew added.

They came past a collection of rocks that looked as if they'd recently been plonked there when in actual fact a glacier had deposited them thousands of years before.

"Shall we take a break?" Andrew said, glancing at an overheating Will.

Beeb came running towards Hardeep with the big stick and the other two dogs stood watching.

"The smallest is the winner," Will laughed. "Nice one, Beeb."

They all sat with their backs to the large rock and took in the valley unfurling below them. Will reached into his pack and got his water. Andrew followed suit. Hardeep looked a bit shamefaced.

"I didn't even think to bring anything."

Will took a swig then handed him his water bottle. "Here you go."

Hardeep took it gratefully. "Thanks. I should have brought something to eat. I didn't even get breakfast today."

Will beamed. He might not be the quickest up the path, but his time to shine had arrived. Out of his pack, he produced a couple of plastic boxes and revealed their contents. He had brought homemade falafel, some vegetable tarts he'd made for his father and sausage rolls. In the other, he had fruit that had gone a bit mushy in the heat but still looked pretty edible.

Hardeep's eyes nearly popped out of their sockets.

Andrew produced a couple of cereal bars out of his pack and threw them down. "My contribution."

"Wow, you guys are on it," Hardeep said.

They dug into the feast with plenty of titbits for the dogs.

"How is life in Napthwaite? Really?" Will asked.

"It's been quite eventful with James, Ed and Arthur scandalising everyone," Hardeep replied.

"Everyone or just my father?" Will said.

Hardeep glanced at Andrew.

"I know what he's like better than anyone," Will continued. "You don't have to tread on eggshells with me."

"Let's say it got a little nasty," Andrew said.

"No doubt we'll go back to the feud between Kathleen Brockbank and Liz soon enough," Hardeep added.

"Imagine there being three gays in this village," Will said.

Andrew sniffed and bit into a slice of apple. "Four actually."

Will had had his suspicions, but Andrew had just laid it out there. "Well, five while I'm here."

Hardeep shifted uncomfortably.

"What brought you to this place?" Will asked Andrew. "Not exactly a haven for us gays, despite the last few weeks."

This time Andrew shifted awkwardly. "Oh, I wanted some peace, so when this reforestation project came up, the timing couldn't have been better."

"Where were you before?" Hardeep asked.

"Down South."

Will couldn't work out if Andrew was being deliberately cagey or if this was just his way. "How long have you been in the village?" he asked Hardeep.

Hardeep leant on the rock. "About fifteen years. We came here when Satinder was a newborn. My wife didn't want to bring her up in the city. Then when we got here, she just moaned endlessly about being bored and I worked all the time. It's a big round. I have to.

Plus she refused to do the shop, so I had to manage everything."

"I guess you just grew apart then?" Andrew added.

"Not quite, but let's just say what we wanted out of life changed."

Will glanced at Andrew. "Whatever led us here, who cares," Will said. "We're here and what a view we've found."

They stopped talking and really took in the rolling hillside, picking out the little farms dotted around and the chimney tops of Holton in the distance.

"I've had a really good time," Hardeep said eventually. "Thank you."

"Me too," Will agreed.

"Me three," Andrew added.

"It's just nice to get out with people my own age. I feel like I've gone back to teenage years. I almost found myself asking Dad if I could go out with my mates."

"Welcome to my world," Hardeep said. "It's not so bad these days. Satinder can be left on her own, but in my day, I had to ask Mum's permission if I wanted to go to the cash and carry."

Andrew stood. He helped Will and Hardeep up. Will marvelled at the way he was literally dragged to his feet by the stronger man. "How about dinner at mine sometime? Since I'm the only boy big enough to have his own place." Andrew grinned.

They set off down the track.

"That would be nice," Will said. "Will it be a cereal bar for every course or can you diversify?"

Andrew swatted him on the head. "Cheek of it."

Hardeep ran past them, shouting as he went, "Last one to the bottom has to wash up after."

Andrew and Will grinned at each other before giving chase.

Chapter Eight

The following weekend, Andrew was Lisa's guest at a work function. One that had more free booze than he'd ever come into contact with.

"I'm absolutely bladdered," Lisa groaned as they made their way unsteadily into their hotel room.

Andrew flopped down on the bed. "Me too. Good night though."

The bed moved and a bottle of wine found its way into his arms.

"Make yourself useful and open that. I need to get out of this bloody outfit."

Andrew knew full well that another drink was absolutely the last thing they needed but he didn't like to argue. He rummaged in his jacket pocket for his Swiss Army Knife keyring and, squinting, he set to work opening the bottle.

"Haven't you done that yet?"

"A little patience please."

"No wonder you can't get a shag if you're this slow."

Andrew stopped battling with the cork and stared into the bathroom. Lisa stood there in her bra and knickers, wiping her makeup off.

"Who says I can't get a shag?"

"Oh, sorry, are you saying you've had a shag?"

Andrew scowled and resumed his attack on the bottle. "I'm not saying that. I'm saying I could if I wanted."

"Sure."

A loud pop declared his victory. A few bits of cork had probably fallen in, but they were both too drunk to care.

Lisa emerged fresh-faced and wrapped in a bathrobe. He handed her the bottle. "Do the honours. I'll get changed."

Unsteadily, he went into the bathroom and changed into his joggers and T-shirt. He didn't possess a pair of pyjamas so when Lisa told him they were staying in a fancy hotel together, this had been the best he could come up with.

By the time he came into the bedroom, a glass of wine had been poured and stood waiting for him on his bedside table.

"Look at me sharing a bed with a rugged tree surgeon," Lisa said as he climbed in.

"I bet you snore. You seem the type."

Lisa playfully swatted him on the arm as he got comfy. "It was wall-to-wall men tonight," she said. "I can't believe nobody took your eye. At last year's Brewers Ball, I ended up with this guy from Cleckheaton. Thighs like slabs of meat."

Andrew shook his head, laughing. "I must have cramped your style tonight."

"I don't mind," Lisa replied. "I'd rather you'd got lucky."

Andrew took a sip of his wine. "I'm not some charity case, you know. I told you, if I wanted a shag, I could get one."

"I bet you haven't had a man over the threshold of that house since you moved in."

Andrew stretched out in the bed. "I'll have you know there are two very handsome men coming round for dinner next weekend."

Lisa raised her head. "Tell me more."

"Nothing more to tell. Two guys I went on a walk with. Yes, one is gay, and the jury is out on the other."

"You dark horse. Going for the old menage like The King's Arms. I'm impressed."

Andrew had started to feel sleepy and just wanted the room to stop the slight spin it had adopted. "It's not all about sex, you know. There's friendship too."

Lisa kissed him on the forehead. "You've got me for that. Get their clothes off."

They both fell fast asleep.

* * * *

A hangover from hell awaited them the next day. They attacked the breakfast buffet with the same level of vigour as they'd attacked the free bar the night before.

Once he'd got home and treated a very indignant Sally to a pig's ear chew, Andrew needed to get things in order. The two guys were coming next week and the house needed a serious clean. Andrew had to admit he had nerves about the whole thing. His cooking skills were nonexistent and now he'd invited a London chef to his house. Plus, he wanted to impress both of them. It had felt so easy on their walk. He might not want any romantic entanglements, but he liked having men around. Lisa had a point—he had spent the last year like some kind of monk. Sally was great, but having some light-hearted banter had been really nice.

After two hours of solid graft in the house, he arrived in front of Thorpe Hall in his Land Rover. He had never been inside the gates of the big house before and took a second to take it in. The dark slate contrasted perfectly with the green and colourful gardens.

The huge oak door opened and Will appeared, sporting a slim-fitting checked shirt and jeans that clung to his toned arse. Andrew's stomach did a flip, which he tried to ignore. Will hauled the door open and got in.

"Howdy," he said.

"Ready?"

"Can't wait."

The Land Rover burst into life and they headed off down the drive. They had set a group chat up, and Will had been complaining about not being able to get decent healthy food for his father. Andrew had offered to drive him to Stockley Bridge's organic supermarket, and Will had jumped at the chance. The countryside whizzed past as they made their way to the town.

"My friend, Lisa, dragged me to the Brewers Ball last weekend. What a weird crowd, all getting overly excited by the head on a pint."

"Not the kind of head you were after then?"

Will might have grown up in these parts, but he had that directness of Londoners that took Andrew by surprise. "Not quite. What have you been up to?"

"I've been going through some of my old things," Will said. "Dad kept everything. Boxes and boxes of it in the end spare room."

"You sound surprised."

"I am a bit. Dad and I haven't always got on that well. I kind of figured he would have thrown it all out."

"My mum keeps everything too." Andrew laughed. "If you went into my bedroom at home, you'd love the pictures she has on the wall. It's like some bloody shrine."

"Aww. I bet you were cute when you were little."

"A podgy kid with red cheeks."

They came into the larger town and parked.

"Are you getting ingredients for Saturday?" Will asked.

Embarrassed, Andrew couldn't meet the eyes of the clearly talented man in front of him. He had tried to find some recipes online, but they all seemed very complicated and he didn't have half the equipment he'd needed for them.

"What's up?"

They walked into the supermarket that had rows of things which Andrew had a vague idea of what they were, but no clue what to actually do with them.

"I'm not the best cook in the world. I thought a pizza and beer night."

Will picked up a basket. "That's a cop-out. I'll do you a deal. You buy the ingredients and I'll do something with them."

Andrew's heart soared. "You mean it?"

"Of course. I never say anything I don't mean."

"You have yourself a deal, my friend."

They spent a companionable hour in the shop. Andrew marvelled at the practiced way Will found the best produce. He squeezed, he smelled and he examined.

"I usually just pick the one nearest to me. You really go for it, don't you?"

Will winked. "You have to have a squeeze to know if it's ripe."

"Is that right?" To Andrew's amazement, his cock twitched. This man had an effect on him and watching him rooting through the courgettes was a sight to behold. He almost regretted that they'd invited Hardeep. The night could go a very different direction if it were just the two of them.

He hadn't slept with anyone since Neil. The thought of him made his anxiety flare. He didn't know if he had got it together enough to sleep with anyone else.

"You okay?" A concerned Will stared at him.

"Me? Yes why?"

"Your face. You looked like you had the weight of the world on your shoulders."

Andrew forced a smile onto his face. "Just thinking. If you're doing a ratatouille, do we have white or red with that?"

"White, of course."

"Oh of course," Andrew said.

"Right, I've got enough to keep my dad out of the hospital for a while. You've got enough to feed an army. Shall we pay?"

They queued up at the checkouts.

"What do you make of Hardeep?" Will asked.

Andrew frowned. "What do you mean?"

"Closet case?"

Will was as bad as Lisa. Andrew must be getting naïve in his old age. He had just seen a man with a daughter and assumed he was straight. "Nah, no way. He was married."

Will pulled a face. "Because that's the ultimate test of someone's straightness. Even Elton John married a woman once upon a time."

They shifted up the queue. Andrew couldn't stop revisiting his conversations with Hardeep to see if there were any clues.

"I can't see it," he decided. "Not everyone is gay."

"Perhaps," Will said. "But in this case, I'd put money on it."

Chapter Nine

"No chance of dinner in the garden then," Hardeep said, dodging another puddle. It had been pouring down all day and the lane had reduced to a muddy mess.

"This poncho is leaking down the back of my neck," Will cried out, shuddering. His bag with three bottles of wine in clanked. To his amazement, Matthew had offered him the choice of his wine cellar. Will had been impressed. Matthew had built up quite a collection that would rival any top-class restaurant in London.

Soon enough, they were shaking out their raincoats and being ushered into Andrew's house.

"Take a seat. Are you dry now?"

Will sat on the sofa, gratefully receiving a huge glass of wine. "Bloody hell, Andrew. I'll be drunk before I even get started."

"Started?" Hardeep said.

Andrew looked a little shamefaced as he stroked Sally.

"Will offered to rustle something up. I'm so crap in the kitchen, I didn't want to risk it."

"Fair enough. I'm terrible too. I've never had to learn, with Mum and after that my wife."

Andrew glanced at him, but Will hadn't changed his mind about Hardeep, and he had every intention to use tonight to find out a bit more about the mysterious postman.

"How is your dad?" Andrew asked.

"Oh, he's doing better every day, thanks. He's started getting up in the afternoon. We watch crappy quiz shows and he makes it a point to beat me."

"You sound like an old married couple," Hardeep said. "Parents, eh? Mum is still watching James and his two men like a hawk. I don't know what she thinks they are going to do."

Will stretched out on the old saggy sofa. It suited the shabby-chic décor of the lounge. Nothing seemed to match, but it all worked perfectly well. Andrew had an eye for it.

"Perhaps she wishes she'd tried the whole threeway thing."

Hardeep threw a cushion at him. "Do you mind?"

Will returned the favour, sending the cushion sailing over the room. "You weren't brought by the stork, you know."

Sally barked at this bizarre game of catch. Will picked up a very chewed ball from the floor and threw it down the room towards the dining table. She dutifully chased it.

"Sorry, Sally. We haven't given you any attention."

She came back, slobbering and deposited the ball at his feet.

"You've started something now," Andrew said. "She won't stop."

Will got up. "I will have to though, or we'll never eat. You two can come and talk to me while I'm cooking."

They went through to the kitchen. Will started to root around in the cupboards. Andrew hadn't been wrong when he'd said he hardly had any equipment. Will had seen student halls with more stuff.

Luckily he'd chosen to make a ratatouille, so all he needed was a pan and a dish. Surely Andrew couldn't fail on that score. Eventually he found some suitable tools and set to chopping.

"Can I help?" Hardeep asked.

"Sure you can. Here, slice up this onion."

Andrew hung around like a spare part. "I feel bad that both my guests are dealing with dinner."

Will winked. "Make yourself useful then. We need top ups and some music."

Andrew scurried into the lounge.

"Do you miss her?" Will asked.

Hardeep frowned. "Who?"

"Your wife."

Hardeep thought about this for a second. "In a way, I guess. We grew up together and would play together all the time. Her family lived about three doors down from us."

Will handed him a pepper. "Can you chop that when you've finished?"

Hardeep resumed his work.

"When did she leave?"

"Oh, years ago. Satinder had only just started school. It's her I feel for more than me. Mum does her best, but there's a generation gap there. She needs a mother."

Andrew came into the room and put the wine glasses down next to them.

"Don't you hear from her?"

"Nah. She met a guy who sold dodgy phones. He ended up with an arrest out for him, and next thing, she rings me to say they are off to Thailand. She never came back. She sends Satinder Christmas and birthday cards. But she wasn't maternal. I wanted kids, not her."

Sally sat at their feet, patiently waiting for anything that might fall to the floor.

"Sorry, girl," Will said. "All veggies tonight. Nothing for you."

"Carrots are her absolute favourites. That's what she's after," Andrew said. He fiddled with his phone and the dulcet tones of Adele burst out of the speakers.

"That's a bit depression-session, isn't it?" Will said "It's a party."

Andrew grumbled. Kylie replaced Adele.

"That's a bit more like it," Hardeep said.

Will handed Sally a carrot, and she promptly went off to her bed to do battle.

"She'll love you forever now," Andrew said with a wink.

"A woman of taste then," Will replied.

Hardeep handed Will the prepared vegetables. He had done a better job than some of the people in the kitchen at Haven.

"I'm impressed."

"Thanks. Mum trained me from birth to be her assistant."

Hardeep took his glass and sat next to Andrew at the table while Will busied himself assembling their dinner.

"Must be hard living with your mum. I don't know how you do it," Andrew said.

Hardeep looked a little bashful. "It's not so bad. She came through for me when I needed her most. I couldn't run a business and bring up a five-year-old. She's a bit full-on, especially once she got on with bloody Kath Brockbank and Mrs Turnbull..."

"Napthwaite's coven," Will laughed.

"You may joke. I have them in my house every Saturday morning. Picking over what's happened in the week."

Nothing much changed in Napthwaite, only the faces. Will could remember his mother telling him the gossips had had a field day when his father had brought home a wife from the Philippines.

He couldn't imagine a defiant Matthew being the talk of the village.

"You'll be a good source of intel then," he said.

Hardeep nodded. "I can reveal that this week, Liz Poole had her windows cleaned at last, Rob and Jenny Holdsworth have booked a holiday to South Africa and David Chan is thinking about having off-street parking."

A pang of guilt stabbed at him. David Chan had been his best friend at school, and he'd been in Napthwaite for three weeks without going round to visit. They had bumped into each other in the street and had a nice catch-up, but he really must do something about it.

Time had turned into a strange medium being with his father. He didn't like to leave him for too long. Mrs Turnbull had offered to come round and play Scrabble with him that night so Will could let his hair down.

"Work must be wanting you back soon?" Hardeep asked.

"Trying to get rid of me?" Will answered in mock outrage.

"No of course not, I just thought—"

"Relax, I'm joking. I got a month off, so I guess I'll have to ring them next week. To tell you the truth, I could live without it. I'd forgotten what life was like without being screamed at morning, noon and night by a prima donna with a whisk."

Hardeep shuddered. "I couldn't face having a boss breathing down my neck again."

Will threw a mushroom at him which he caught and popped in his mouth. "Bragger."

"Have a heart. I've an overbearing mother and a stroppy teenager in my house. I think I'm allowed a pass on a nasty boss."

"Sounds like you're a bit lost in all that," Andrew said.

The smile dropped from Hardeep's face. "I guess it does. I think I've been lost for so long I've forgotten who I am."

"You could find him again, I'm sure," Andrew continued.

Hardeep thought for a second. "I suppose. I might be scared at who I'd find though. I don't know, freedom was never really on the cards for me. That's fine. I'm happy with my lot."

Will glanced at Andrew and raised an eyebrow.

"*Told you,*" he mouthed as Hardeep resumed preparing the vegetables.

Chapter Ten

The feast before them made Hardeep's mouth water. "You've spoilt us," he said.

"Oh, it's nothing. Just chopping and heating."

Hardeep glanced at Andrew who blew furiously on a steaming forkful before putting in his mouth. He closed his eyes as he chewed.

"So good."

Will sat next to Hardeep, who filled his glass. "Thanks."

"You're not just a pretty face after all," Andrew said with a wink.

He might not be an expert, but Hardeep could see when two people were flirting. He felt like a spare wheel and wondered to himself why they'd invited him. He took a bite of the food, but his appetite had left him.

"You all right there?" Will asked.

Hardeep tried to put a brave face on. "Yes, I'm fine. This is wonderful. Thank you."

Will frowned but carried on with his meal.

The rain still pelted against the window, which gave it an almost winter's feel even though they were still in August.

"So, Hardeep. No Mrs Kaur mark two on the horizon?" Andrew asked.

Hardeep focused on the food in front of him. "No thanks. My mother and my daughter are enough for me."

"I don't blame you," Andrew continued. "That beautiful lady over there is my world."

Sally glanced up from her bed before resting her head.

"Do you have a man in London, Will?" Hardeep asked.

"Nah," Will said. "I've given up on dates. They always end in disaster."

"What a trio we are," Hardeep said. He wanted to get back his happy vibe that he'd started the evening with. "I'm sure they don't all end in disaster though."

Will looked thoughtful for a second. "I tried to get my act together in the spring. I thought I'd hit the old apps. Firstly, I met Paul who complained about going on dates because he always ends up, and I quote, having drinks with wankers. Then Gordon who spent twenty minutes telling me all about his recycling bins and what days they went out."

Hardeep and Andrew were in fits of laughter.

"Oh, and special mention to Jonathan, who told me we couldn't sleep together because our star signs weren't compatible. I'm sorry, but I refuse to believe that I can't have sex with a twelfth of the population."

Andrew wiped a tear from his eye. "Yes, they sound like disaster. You must have the pick of the crop, so I fear it might be your choosing skills."

"Pick of the crop? I wish."

"Come off it. You must know you're drop-dead gorgeous."

Will shifted in his seat. "That must be good wine."

"Hardeep, tell him," Andrew said.

"Andrew is right," Hardeep said. "You are very handsome."

"You two do wonders for a boy's confidence. So come on, Andrew. What about you?"

Hardeep noticed a change in expression on Andrew's face. It wasn't that he got cross, but a dark cloud definitely washed over him.

"Dating hasn't been my thing for a while. Bit of a bad relationship."

Will didn't seem to be perturbed by this. "Sorry to hear that. I guess it happens to the best of us."

"Yeah."

Hardeep took a large swig of his wine. It had definitely gone to his head. "Want to know something?" he said.

Will and Andrew both looked up eagerly.

"Always," Will said.

"I've only ever had sex with my wife."

Both men sat with open mouths.

"But…" Andrew said.

Realisation dawned on Will's face. "She left ten years ago."

Hardeep shrugged his shoulders and carried on eating.

"Let me get this straight," Andrew said. "You haven't had sex in ten years?"

When he heard it out loud, it did sound pretty awful. However, the shocked faces in front of him made him giggle. "There's more to life," he replied.

"That's as may be, Hardeep," Will said. "But it's still a good part of it."

"It's been a year for me," Andrew offered up.

Will's head shot round. "A year? Bloody hell."

"I thought you said you weren't doing dating anymore," Hardeep said.

"I'm not, but that's why God invented the gay sauna. Bloody hell. I thought I was doing well at managing a few months."

Hardeep had heard of these places. They had a couple in Leeds. He'd even plucked up the courage to find out where and drive past. But he had never been in. He couldn't risk someone in his family seeing him coming out.

He marvelled at the free way that these two were able to share their sex lives. It had never been talked about in his home. He and his wife had had to resort to watching porn to even work out what to do.

He put his knife and fork down on his plate. "That was absolutely incredible, Will. Thank you so much."

Will waved him away.

"Shall we sit comfy?" Andrew said, ushering them over to the two big sofas by the inglenook fireplace.

Hardeep sat on one and Will and Andrew sat on the other.

"You two are so free," he said. "I wish I could be more like that. You make me feel like I've missed out."

Will shook his head. "Babe, you've got a beautiful daughter, a business and a future. You've nothing to feel worried about."

He supposed the grass always did look greener. He had spent the last ten years working to not only keep the post office afloat but to make it thrive. He stocked all sorts of oddments that villagers had come to rely on.

"Love isn't all it's cracked up to be, anyway," Andrew piped up. "It can nearly kill you."

Will caught Hardeep's eye, but neither of them seemed to want to interrogate Andrew further. He had been in a funny mood since they'd mentioned this.

Andrew changed the music. The chilled tunes of Goldfrapp filled the room like a breath of fresh air.

Will suddenly sat up. "Hardeep. I've a question."

Hardeep shuddered. "Go on."

"If you've only ever had sex with your wife...how do you know she was any good?"

He had never thought about that before. Perhaps he had never had good sex. She'd soon run off...had his prowess been the thing that had driven her away?

How could he admit that to these two gorgeous and experienced men?

"I never enjoyed it. I just wanted a child."

He saw Will and Andrew exchange a glance. Andrew filled their glasses up. Hardeep would have to stop soon—the booze had gone to his head.

"Do you think it's that you don't like sex or just not with her?" Will continued.

They were backing him into a corner. "Perhaps with her. I don't know."

Andrew moved so he perched on the edge of the sofa. "Do you think it's just because it wasn't like this?" He leant forward and kissed Will.

The kiss started lightly but soon accelerated. Andrew ran his hand up Will's neck and to the back of his head. Will ran his hand over Andrew's biceps.

Hardeep sat there, transfixed. His cock hardening but he couldn't move. The two men panted now as they came up for air.

Andrew looked across at Hardeep.

"I should go," Hardeep said.

"Don't," Will said. "We were only messing."

Andrew stretched, making no attempt to hide his erection inside his shorts. "You know what?" he said. "I reckon we should take this into the bedroom."

Adrenalin rushed through Hardeep's body. He had thought about this so many times with different men. *Can I be this brave?*

Will glanced at Andrew and nodded. "Fuck it, why not?"

They both looked Hardeep again.

"Why don't you come with us?" Will asked. "It will be more fun with three."

"I don't know…"

"You can stay in the spare room if you prefer or make a run for it. The rain has stopped. But I'd rather you came with us," Andrew added.

Hardeep couldn't speak.

Andrew got up and held his hand out to Will, who took it. They both walked over to the doorway that led to the stairs.

The night had taken a hell of a turn, and Hardeep thought his heart could burst out of his chest then and there.

"We might see you in a minute, then?" Will said.

"Yeah," Hardeep said with a nervous giggle.

They left him sitting in the lounge on his own. Their footsteps could be heard on the stairs leading into what must be a room above him. The old beams creaked, signalling weight had settled on a bed.

Sally stared across at him.

"Oh fuck," Hardeep said to himself. "What do I do now?"

Chapter Eleven

The clock seemed to tick louder. The music on the stereo seemed to taunt him. His heart couldn't stop hammering ten to the dozen. Hardeep sat for a second more before standing.

The front door dominated his view. It would be so easy to just open it and walk out. His mum would be knitting away at home and his daughter lazing on the sofa watching TV. They probably wouldn't even ask if he'd had a nice time.

But will I ever forgive myself? Upstairs lay his chance to experience what he'd thought about most of his life. Will and Andrew had obviously rumbled him long before tonight, which was why they'd kept asking him.

He worried that he'd given them far too much insight into his life. If they could see, could everyone else?

Above him the beams creaked.

He caught sight of himself in the huge pine mirror above the fireplace, then, with a deep breath, set off across the room and up the stairs. At the top of the stairs he could see the light under the door. All was quiet in the room now.

He swallowed hard and pushed the door open.

Will and Andrew were sitting up in bed, the duvet just covering their waists.

"About bloody time," Will said. "I thought you were going to leave us hanging for a second."

Hardeep smiled shyly. "I did too." He felt stupid standing there like a spare part.

"Well, get your kit off and get in here, then," Andrew said.

He dragged the duvet off, exposing their naked bodies. Will lay with his legs slightly apart. His slim waist formed a V that led down to his hard, thick cock and his tanned, hairless body had a tattoo on the arm.

Andrew's muscular build looked incredible. His toned pecs were covered in the same blond hair that was on his head and his six-pack led down to the biggest cock Hardeep had ever seen — and that included porn. Andrew absentmindedly stroked it.

But the warm expressions on both men's faces told Hardeep he could do this. They were inviting him, not scorning him.

He unbuttoned his shirt and threw it off. He knew they would be taking in his thick hairy chest and slim waist. He kicked off his shoes and dropped his trousers. He had good legs. Anyone would with the post round he did daily.

His cock pressed at the black boxer shorts. He dropped them to the floor, pulling off his socks at the same time. Will held his hand out for him and Hardeep went to him. He went to sit on the side of the bed, but Andrew and Will parted, leaving space in between them.

"Oh no, the guest of honour goes here." Andrew laughed.

Tentatively, Hardeep crawled in between them. The feeling of heat from both their bodies on either side of him was an experience he had never dreamt of before.

Will reached across and ran his hand through Hardeep's thick chest hair before resting on his nipple.

Andrew, in turn, stroked Hardeep's torso, making him twitch, then moved across to settle on Will's waist.

"Your heart is going like a machine gun," Will said.

"Just a bit nervous is all."

Andrew nuzzled into his neck. The wisps of his blond locks tickled against Hardeep's face. "Nothing to be nervous of."

Will moved his hand up Hardeep's body and faced him. Then he leant in and kissed him.

Hardeep thought he might burst. The touch of Will's lips, the graze of his stubble, the big hands starting to roam over his body from both sides—he had wanted this his whole life but never in his wildest dreams thought it would happen like this.

Will pushed his tongue into his mouth, exploring gently. Hardeep followed suit. His nerves drifted away as he got used to the smell and feel of the two men. A finger on his chin drew him away from Will's kiss and straight into Andrew's much hungrier mouth. Now Hardeep had become confident enough to match him.

Hardeep ran his hand through Andrew's thick hair that smelt of the forests he worked in. Will was behind him, his breath on his ears as he nuzzled into him.

Will moved on the bed. Hardeep broke the kiss to watch him as he took Andrew's cock in his mouth, looking up at them both while he licked up to the head. Andrew moaned, kissing Hardeep's neck.

"Oh yeah," he murmured.

Hardeep's cock ached. This was incredible. Will caught his eye as he teased the end of Andrew's cock with his tongue.

Andrew writhed in anticipation now. Hardeep felt Andrew's muscular chest and down to his stomach.

Will didn't wait any longer and took Andrew's whole cock in his mouth. Andrew let out a shout of pleasure, making Will move up and down the shaft. Andrew greedily turned to Hardeep for more kisses, which he gladly supplied.

Andrew softly caressed Hardeep's back and into his hair as Will worked on him. Will's other hand encased his cock and gently massaged.

His heart had stopped pounding quite so much but he still couldn't believe this was happening to him. Will crawled up Andrew's body and all three mouths met. Hardeep pulled away as Will and Andrew became lost in the kiss. Andrew wrapped his legs around Will's waist which ground against his own.

They rolled over so that Andrew straddled Will, kissing him. Hardeep watched their cocks nestling together as Andrew leant back. He wrapped his hand around them both and gently tugged, making Will close his eyes. Hardeep froze for a second. Glancing from one to the other, he rubbed his own cock.

Andrew bucked his hips so his and Will's cocks slid in and out of his hand. The anxiety returned to Hardeep like a sledgehammer and he got off the bed. Will and Andrew stopped what they were doing.

"Are you okay, H?" Will said.

"Yeah. No. I don't know." He perched on the end of the bed.

Andrew moved across to him and put his hands on his shoulders, drawing him in slightly so Hardeep's back leant against his warm, muscular chest. "What's the matter?"

Will scrambled off the bed and kneeled on the floor in front of Hardeep. He placed his hands on his knees and squeezed them. "Is this not for you? It's okay to say."

He had no doubt he wanted this so badly. So why had he frozen? "I never thought in my wildest dreams I would find myself in a situation like this. But you two, well, you're so experienced. I don't know anything."

Will ran his hands up his legs. "It's not some kind of test."

"We've all been in this position," Andrew said, squeezing him tight. "It's fine."

"But if you want to go, you can," Will added. "No judgement."

He had absolutely no intention of leaving. He wanted to break through his barriers and enjoy himself. "Not at all. I'm just feeling a bit overwhelmed."

Will stood. Hardeep marvelled at his body and reached forward to touch his hips. He took hold of Will's hard cock. Will moaned. Hardeep examined it slowly. Pre-cum glistened on the end. Could he do this?

"Just go for it," Andrew whispered in his ear.

It was all the encouragement Hardeep needed. He leant forward and took Will's cock in his mouth. He might not be as expert as the other two, but the feel of it lived up to what he had imagined all those nights alone.

"Oh, yeah," Will murmured.

Giving a gorgeous man like this pleasure made Hardeep's spine tingle. He slowly moved his mouth up and down the length of Will's hard cock. Once he came up for air, he smiled at Will.

"Why is he the bloody favourite?" Andrew protested.

Hardeep turned around as Andrew lay on the bed. Hardeep looked down at the much bigger dick awaiting his attention. He took this one in his mouth too. It took a second to get used to the size, but he mastered it and soon had Andrew's hips bucking as he worked it.

Will leant down next to him and they took turns licking Andrew's hard shaft. He squirmed and moaned in response.

Hardeep wrapped his fingers around the base and pumped. Will put his fingers over Hardeep's and they moved in time together. They kissed.

"What a fucking view," Andrew sighed as they worked his cock, Hardeep matching Will's speed. "Oh God, I'm going to come."

Andrew's muscular frame tensed as he let out a cry, his cum shooting up his body and over their hands.

"Come here," he panted.

They kneeled on either side of him. He gently curled his fingers around their cocks, one in each hand.

"Come on me," Andrew instructed, tugging each of their cocks.

Hardeep gripped the headboard. He was so turned on he wouldn't take long. Will grabbed Hardeep by the back of the neck and kissed him hard.

Hardeep let himself go, caressing Andrew's sticky body below them as he glided past the point of no return.

He came first, the orgasm gripping him. Seconds later, Will's body tensed and his breathing become laboured.

Breaking the kiss, he watched Will's cum joining his own and Andrew's.

He resumed kissing Will while their heartrates returned to normal. They broke the kiss and Hardeep grinned at both of them.

"Wow."

Chapter Twelve

Will lay with his head on Andrew's chest, Hardeep cuddled into his side. The afterglow felt great. Their bodies slotted against one another as if they'd been designed for that purpose.

"I didn't expect things to turn out like that," Hardeep said.

Andrew played Hardeep's hair. "Really? I think I had a suspicion."

Hardeep lifted his head up. "Did you?"

"Come on. It's been pretty obvious we've been attracted to each other."

Will's heart soared at the adorable look of confusion on Hardeep's face. He leant his head up and kissed Hardeep. "You have no idea how gorgeous you are."

Hardeep bashfully put his head back down on the pillow. "Sorry for having a bit of a wobble," he said.

Will snuggled into him. "There's nothing to apologise for. It's not some test about how well you perform. We had a nice time together — there's nothing wrong in that."

"I had a great time," Andrew said. "I bloody needed that. You two can visit again."

Will agreed wholeheartedly. The last month had been stressful. "It makes a change to have sex with someone I care about," he said. "The saunas are convenient, but I really like you two. I've wanted it since I saw you chatting on the street."

Hardeep sat up. "You can show me everything. We could be the Wednesday night club."

"I like the sound of that. Lisa is always on at me to join something to get to know the villagers," Andrew said. "This is what she meant, right?"

"Then we fall merrily in love and live happily ever after," Will laughed.

"We could combine with The King's Arms and have a Christmas party," Hardeep added.

They were both giggling.

"Instead of keys in a fruit bowl, we could have names in a stocking," Will countered.

"Careful, you're getting me hard again," Hardeep added.

Andrew extracted himself from Will's arms and got up off the bed. He looked very serious and picked up his boxer shorts from the floor. "Can't believe it's nearly ten. I'd better take Sally out."

Will sat up. "We should leave you to it then."

"Yeah, sorry. Do you mind?"

Will and Hardeep got up off the bed, shooting each other a confused glance.

"Of course not."

They all dressed in silence. The change in mood had totally broadsided Will and he suspected Hardeep felt the same.

When they got downstairs, Sally sat expectantly at the door.

"Right, well thanks for a great evening," Hardeep said.

"Yes, it's been lovely," Will added.

Andrew was making a big deal of finding a coat under the stairs. "Definitely. Thank you for cooking, Will."

Hardeep opened the door and he and Will walked out into the warm summer night air. "See you then."

Andrew stood in the doorway. Will went forward to kiss him, but he took a step back, leaving Will feeling stupid. "Bye."

They turned and set off down the lane. Once out of earshot, Will let out a sigh. "Weird ending to the night."

"I'll say," Hardeep said, worry in his voice. "Did we make a mistake?"

Will rested his hand on Hardeep's shoulder. "Not the sex. Chill out. I meant Andrew practically throwing us out."

They got to the bottom of the road. A car drove past into the village and Hardeep instinctively pulled away from him.

"Relax. They wouldn't have even seen us."

"Sorry."

"Come here."

Will led him over to a wall that had a tree growing just to the side. The ground was still soggy from the rain before, but the wall seemed dry enough. They sat on it and Will took Hardeep's hand in his own. "I know that tonight has been a massive deal for you. Please don't second-guess any of it. You were great. For the record, it's true that I've wanted to do that since I saw you both on the street. Plus I want to do it again."

Hardeep leant forward and kissed him. "Me too. Although it will probably be just us two. I don't think Andrew will want it again."

"If that's the case, then so be it. But he'll be the one missing out. We've only just touched the surface of your education."

The silence of the night made the whole thing feel so clandestine and horny. He kissed Hardeep again and ran his hand up his leg. When he reached the top, he could feel Hardeep's erection. "Stand against that tree and drop your trousers."

"I can't…"

"Yes, you can."

Hardeep hesitated for a second before a grin appeared on his face. He leapt off the wall and moved over to the tree. Slowly he unbuttoned his trousers and let them fall to the floor.

"Now the undies."

Hardeep ran his finger along the waistband before pulling them down. His cock sprang up, hard and solid.

Will licked his lips. It had all got a bit frantic at Andrew's. This time he wanted to savour it. He squatted down, his face level with the swollen dick in front of him and took it all in his mouth. Hardeep groaned. Will placed his hands gently on Hardeep's hips and moved him in time. Hardeep got the message and began fucking Will's mouth.

Will reached down and fiddled with his fly. Reaching inside, he squeezed his cock. Hardeep rested his hands on the top of Will's head as he drove his cock in and out of his mouth. "Oh yeah, Will."

Will sucked as hard as he could. Hardeep grabbed hold of Will's head, bucking his hips faster. Then he let out a moan and his hot salty liquid invaded Will's mouth. He swallowed it down and looked up at Hardeep. "You taste amazing," he said, standing and kissing Hardeep. "See?"

Hardeep licked his lips and kissed Will again. Will pressed his body up against him and Hardeep reached inside Will's trousers.

Will couldn't get enough. This man had the lightest touch that gave him shudders. "Make me come," he whispered.

Hardeep didn't need any further encouragement. He slowly but steadily massaged Will's cock as they resumed the kiss. This time more frantic as he built Will up to the inevitable crescendo.

Will put his hand behind Hardeep's head, leaning on the gnarly bark of the tree. His breath coming in fits and starts as he lost himself in the feeling. Then he threw his head back, staring up at the moon as the orgasm washed over him. "Oh yeah, Jesus you're good at that."

Spent, they both put their clothes back on properly.

"I don't want to go home," Hardeep said. "Shame we got thrown out."

They hopped over the wall and resumed their walk home. The village clock struck ten. Crowds were spilling out of The King's now the rain had stopped. Suddenly both their phones bleeped.

"No prizes for guessing who this is," Hardeep said.

A message had come through on the group chat.

Sorry for the abrupt finish. I have baggage. Cum again soon, A x

Will thought about what to say when he saw Hardeep furiously typing. *We just did x*

"Couldn't have put it better myself."

Their phones went again.

Without me? Damn

This time Will started to type. *Snooze you lose, big boy. Don't worry, you can lead Hardeep's next lesson x*

Hardeep followed his lead. *I promise to do everything you tell me*

They carried on walking. The phone bleeped.

"He's regretting it now," Will said with a smirk.

They opened their screen to see a naked pic of Andrew on the bed with a sad face.

Hardeep frowned. "Maybe he wants us to go back."

Will agreed with him but he didn't like being practically thrown out of a house, no matter what the baggage was. "He can want. You need to learn that you don't always give everyone what they want, Hardeep. Then when they get it, they value it more."

They were at the bridge where they had to part.

Hardeep stared at him for a second. "If we're supposed to leave people wanting more, shouldn't you have left me on the edge at the tree?"

Skewered by his own words. Will had been about to admit defeat when a thought struck. He moved closer so a hair's breadth separated them. "How about you think about me riding up and down that rock-hard cock of yours next time we meet? Maybe even think about having Andrew's dick in your mouth at the same time. Is that leaving you wanting more?"

Hardeep nodded. They glanced around and stole a quick kiss before Hardeep set off towards Queen Street and Will walked towards Thorpe Hall. He turned to see Hardeep walk round the corner.

This had definitely been one of his better dinner parties and he didn't even have to do the washing-up.

Chapter Thirteen

He had been full of regrets after the two had left and even worse when he found out they had carried on without him.

"You only have yourself to blame," Lisa said. She had her feet up on his lap as they watched some drama on Netflix about a group of people avoiding being murdered for not playing childhood games correctly.

He couldn't even argue with her. "I know. Fuck knows what's wrong with me."

"I think you probably do know. Deep down."

Once again, he had no comeback for this. She had been desperate for him to open up to her ever since they'd met, but he didn't want to open that box. It had been firmly shut over a year ago, and it terrified him to look inside again.

"Something did happen to me before I came here. Something truly awful. But I just can't talk about it, Lisa. I'm sorry."

She pressed pause on the remote control. "You don't have to apologise. I know I push you and yes, I'm a nosey cow, but I also care about you."

"I will sort myself out."

She got up off the sofa and went into the kitchen, returning with a couple of bottles of beer. "Here, I brought you some freebies."

He'd had a lot the night before, but Andrew didn't like to turn down a gift. She opened them up and poured them into their glasses.

"I'm here for you, whatever has happened or happens. You've nothing to worry. But let's face it, poor Mr Willy has been neglected and I can't help you there. Don't fuck this up with these two. It sounds promising to me."

"I think you might be right, you know."

"Tell me about them."

He gathered his thoughts. He had no idea where to start. "Will is fit. His mother was from the Philippines and his father is Napthwaite through and through."

"Interesting combination."

He thought about Will's soft skin, dark hair and toned, firm arse that Andrew hadn't spent half as much time on as he would like. "He's really sweet. I scared poor Hardeep to death at first. He would have run a mile if it had been just me and him. But Will put him at ease. He's a special guy."

"And Hardeep?"

"Oh, he's absolutely gorgeous. Haven't you seen him on his rounds?"

"Only from afar."

Hardeep had no idea the power he possessed in his looks. That made him all the more irresistible. "He's not come out of his shell yet."

Lisa took a swig of her beer. "What a head fuck. You go for dinner with your two new mates and find out their dicks are dessert. I bet he's been wanking all day."

"Bloody hell, Lisa."

"Well, you sound like some kind of Mills and Boon novel. Give me the real details."

He shook his head. "Not a chance. Some things are a secret."

Lisa pondered this for a second. "Well, I wish you all the best. This sounds like it could be a whole lot of fun for you."

The glint in her eye amused him. "Plus it makes good gossip for you."

"And that, too. The marketing guy is a dud. I've had to give him the heave-ho."

He frowned. "I thought you said he was the best thing ever."

"He shouted for his mother when he came," she said indignantly.

The words hung there for a second before Andrew exploded into laughter. "What the fuck?"

She shook her head and they giggled until their sides hurt. Then when they caught each other's eyes, the mirth would all start again.

"Never in my forty years on this planet have I ever heard anything so gross."

Lisa wiped her eye with her sleeve. "You try being underneath it."

"What did you do?"

"I got rid, of course."

"I'm going to tell Will and Hardeep about that one. It might make them think I'm not so weird."

Lisa put her feet on his lap. "Glad to be of service. But I mean it, Andrew. Don't fuck this up by overthinking it. It doesn't have to be anything you don't want it to be. You're in control of your own life."

He squeezed her foot. He found it hard to believe they had only known each other for a year. How had he managed before her? They binge-watched the programme into the night before stumbling upstairs to bed, full of talk about who should have died and who shouldn't.

"You getting in with me?"

"Have you changed the sheets?"

"Erm…"

"Night then."

Lisa went into the spare room and shut the door. Sally wasn't as fussy and had leapt up on the bed by the time he came out of the bathroom. He could still smell Hardeep and Will. They filled his thoughts as they had for most of the day. He snuggled under the duvet and switched off the light. Before he drifted off to sleep, he made a vow to make amends for the ridiculous way he'd finished the evening with Will and Hardeep.

* * * *

Of course they both slept in, and he awoke to the sound of Lisa swearing that she had a meeting in less than an hour. He opened his eyes sleepily to see her fully dressed at the foot of his bed.

"I'm going."

"One sec. I'll wave you off." He leapt out of bed and remembered just in time he didn't have any clothes on.

"Bloody hell, Andrew. Let a girl have a coffee before you start waving that thing around."

He quickly grabbed his bathrobe and covered himself up. "Sorry."

They dashed down the stairs.

"You'll have no trouble getting them back. I can guarantee," Lisa said.

"Do you want a coffee?"

She dithered for a second, which was interrupted by a knock on the door. Sally started barking as per usual.

"Fucking hell, it's all happening this morning," Andrew grumbled. His heart leapt when he opened the door and saw Hardeep on the step.

"Morning. Post for you." Hardeep's smile faltered when he saw Lisa.

"Don't mind me. I'll skip that coffee. Better go." She pushed past Hardeep and out onto the garden path. "Have fun, boys."

Hardeep turned to Andrew. "Did you tell her?"

They hadn't discussed not telling people, but it suddenly occurred to Andrew that Hardeep was still firmly in the closet. "She won't tell anyone. I promise."

"Bloody hell, Andrew. I wish I could have had a say in that."

Andrew ushered Hardeep in and pulled the bathrobe tighter round him. "I'm fucking up at every opportunity, aren't I?"

Poor Hardeep didn't look like he knew what to do at all. He ran his hands through his hair. "It's fine. She's not from Napthwaite. I recognise her, though."

"She owns the brewery in Holton."

Andrew went into the kitchen and flicked the kettle on. He was dealing with a lot before his first coffee, which didn't sit well with him at all. "I'm sorry, Hardeep. I ruined Wednesday night and now I've upset you again."

Hardeep stood in the doorway. He looked cute in his postman uniform of pale blue shirt and dark blue shorts. "You didn't ruin Wednesday. Are you kidding? I had the best night ever."

"I ruined the end."

Hardeep shrugged. "Let's say it came to an abrupt halt. We can make up for it."

Andrew perked up at the suggestion that he hadn't shoved Hardeep so far back into the closet he'd found Narnia. "So you'd want to do it again?"

Hardeep came into the kitchen. "Most definitely. I've still a lot to learn and I think I've found my two teachers."

Andrew kissed him. "And Lisa?"

"Not a lot we can do about that now, is there?"

"I'll do better."

Hardeep slid his hand inside Andrew's bathrobe and found his cock. He encircled it and squeezed gently, spurring it into action. Andrew sighed as he hardened in Hardeep's palm.

"Oh God."

Hardeep dropped to his knees and yanked open Andrew's robe. He ran his lips over the hard shaft.

Andrew might have been woken rudely by Lisa, but if it meant a happy ending like this, he was more than on board. Hardeep took his whole cock in his mouth, sliding it in and out as Andrew gripped the kitchen counter. Suddenly, Hardeep let his cock fall out of his mouth and stood.

"What the…?"

"Until next time," Hardeep said with a wink.

Without even waiting for a reply, he turned and walked out of the house.

I'm learning all right.

Chapter Fourteen

Another heated debate on where Titus should sleep had sent Matthew and Will into separate corners of the house. Matthew, who grew stronger by the day, had decided to listen to his classical music at maximum volume.

Will hid in his old room, sorting through photos. He had really enjoyed discovering the pictures of his mother. The ones he had in London were imprinted on his memory and it felt like seeing her again, discovering these new shots. His mobile rang. With a sigh, he pressed the Answer button. "Hello, Anton."

"Is this Will Johnstone? Forgive me, I've not heard his voice in so long."

Still the comedian.

"I'm sorry I haven't been in touch. Things have got a bit hectic here." He flinched at the fake laugh on the other side.

"Strange that. I thought I was the busy one. Not having my assistant for practically the whole of August."

September would roll around next week. Surprisingly, Will had no desire to return to London. He and Matthew might have more ups and downs than the rollercoaster at Blackpool Pleasure Beach, but he had settled into a groove in Napthwaite.

"I will come back soon. We did say a month."

"Which is up in a week. I'm doing the rotas and I need to know when to put you on."

Will's head swam. "Next Saturday," he said, just to keep Anton from losing his temper.

"You'd better be here," Anton said. "You're not convincing me."

Rubbing his eyes, he thought about walking into the restaurant as if nothing had happened. The thought of leaving Andrew and Hardeep would be difficult. They had just got it together and now he would bail out. Plus his father had responded so well to him being here, regardless of his protestations.

"I'll be there."

"Have you...uh...have you spoken to HR?"

Interesting that this still rattled Anton. He must really be in the shit. "Not yet. I've got a teleconference with them next week."

Anton took a deep breath. "Tell you what. I'll put you on the shift from a week on Wednesday. Let you ease in. A bit mean to expect you to do a Saturday night after a break."

It amazed him how Anton didn't care about being totally obvious. "That's very generous of you, thank you."

"How is your father by the way?"

Now he asks. "He's doing very well."

"Good stuff. Right. I had better go. We will see you next Wednesday."

"You will."

Will terminated the call and looked at the photos that he had spread across the floor in front of him. The idea of London seemed alien already. What had Napthwaite done to him? With a need to be grounded he pressed Call on his phone. "Ange?"

"Well, hello there, stranger," she replied.

He'd neglected her while he'd been in the North. They'd messaged a few times, but he'd been a bad friend.

"How's tricks?" he said.

"They're good. How are things up there?"

Will sighed. He didn't really have an answer for this. How could he tell her that he had relaxed for the first time in months, maybe years? "Oh, you know. Dad resents me being here."

"Are you glad you went, though?"

"Yeah. Bloody Anton just rang. He wants me on shift next week."

"And you don't want to?"

"I don't. I thought I'd be desperate to get back, but the only person I want to see is you."

She didn't respond. He had never known her lost for words before. "Ange?"

"Ready for another bombshell?"

He gripped the phone tighter. "Oh God, what?"

"I was going to tell you when I saw you in person. Remember that job I went for?"

"In New York?"

"Well, I got it."

His stomach dropped but he gathered himself together. He had to encourage her. This job was all she had ever wanted. "That's great news."

"Say it again. Once more with feeling."

"No, I mean it. Honest I do. It's just…"

"I know, you'll miss my knickers drying on the bathroom radiator."

A lump formed in his throat. She had been the only shining light for him going home, and now she would be on the other side of the Atlantic. Life seemed to be changing at the speed of light suddenly. "Of course I'll miss you."

"I'll miss you too. Unless…"

He frowned. "Unless what?"

"Come with me, Will. You fucking hate Anton. Imagine us two on the loose in the Big Apple. It would be amazing. There are plenty of restaurants there. I'm sure one of them wouldn't mind your shit cooking."

Can I do that? She had a point. He did hate Anton and London had become stale. Could New York be the next credible move for him? "I can't say I'm not tempted."

"Don't be tempted — just do it. Tell Anton to shove it up his fat arse."

"Let me think about it, yeah? I'd have to be sure Dad could cope without me."

"No rush. You can follow me. Let me get a flat, sorry, *apartment*, first. Then you can lodge with me, and I can get revenge for all the times you've nagged me to hang my wet towels up."

They both laughed. It had been a constant struggle to get her to do that. His thoughts were disturbed by a loud knock on the heavy door. "There's someone at the door, love. I'd better go. I will think about it."

"I'm leaving in a couple of weeks. Don't worry — I'll make sure all the towels are washed and dried."

There was another knock.

"Hang on, what are you doing with all your stuff?"

"Going into storage, babe."

"I've got to go. I'll ring you in a day or so." He finished the call and went down to answer the persistent knocking.

James Durkin from The King's Arms stood on the doorstep.

"Hello, Will."

"James. What can we do for you?"

He still had those handsome good looks from school. Will had had such a crush on him.

"I wondered if your dad was up to a visit?"

Will frowned. "He is. I don't want to come across all protective, but can you let me know what it's about?"

James sighed. "It's a tough one."

Will showed him into the entrance hall. James looked around, taking it all in.

"Go on."

"I'm here in my capacity as chair of the parish council. Obviously, your dad has sat on the council for a long time but…"

"You want to know if he can continue."

James' whole face relaxed. "Yes."

Will ran his hands through his hair. He couldn't argue that his father had improved since he'd been home, but he also knew how worked up Matthew got at these meetings. If Will had to go to London, he didn't want to leave him with any unnecessary pressure. "I can't let you upset him like that, James. Is there no way it can wait?"

James shook his head. "I'd love to say yes, but we have to fill the vacancy. If it's a matter of a few more weeks or even a month, I could probably swing it. But if it's going to be longer, then we have to accept he's no longer well enough."

Anger rushed through him. "After everything he's done for this village, you're going to throw him out like this. Just because he's ill?"

James reddened.

"Is this because he turned on you, Ed and Arthur?"

The shock on James' face told Will he had overstepped the mark.

"How can you say that? I'm not going to lie and say that he didn't hurt us, but I would never…"

The anger hadn't left him.

"So you're saying he either puts his health at risk by returning to your stupid council or gives it all up?" He couldn't bear to hear his father being cast aside but equally James must be finding this difficult.

"I'm saying we need a fully fit council member. If he could commit to November or even December at a push."

"It's out of the question."

"What's out of the question?"

Will turned round to see his father coming down the staircase.

"James? What brings you here?"

James shifted uneasily and glanced at Will.

"Dad. James is here about the parish council."

Matthew had reached the bottom of the stairs and had to lean on the banister to catch his breath. Still very frail, he seemed to be making a real effort. Will's heart went out to him.

"I've served on the council for twenty years and it's been my pleasure. I was there when your father led it and was honoured to take his place, even for a short time."

Will remembered when James had beaten Matthew in the election. Things had been thrown and he'd had to listen to the whole story over lunch in London. At the time, he'd been bored and counting the minutes until he could leave. Now he realised how much it had meant to his father and the guilt washed over him.

"And you've been a very valued member, Matthew," James said.

"There's been many a time you'd have cheerfully got rid of me."

James shifted uncomfortably. "I wouldn't go that far. I've disagreed with you, but that's the way life runs."

Matthew nodded and stood next to Will, leaning on him ever so slightly. "I've had quite the learning curve in the last month, and I've been like a bear with a sore head. My son has been wonderful, and I honestly don't believe I'd be stood here if he hadn't come to my rescue."

The anger that had lodged in Will's throat was replaced by a lump. He couldn't look at Matthew as he knew he would burst into tears.

"And I know how much it will have taken you to come here today, James. We may not see eye to eye on a lot of things, but you do this village proud all in all. Even with your…unusual lifestyle."

Will and James locked eyes.

"So I'll fall on my sword. My reign in Napthwaite is over and I'm not too proud to admit that. You'd better have an election and let's hope this village chooses wisely."

Matthew relaxed against Will, and he instinctively reached for him, but Matthew moved away and towards his study.

"I'll let Will show you out."

They watched him go into the room and the classical music album that had finished, resumed. Will nodded to the door and they both walked out onto the drive.

James turned, his face a mix of emotions. "I really am sorry, Will. I dreaded coming up here today. Your father and I have had our differences, but I respect him."

"Come on. I'll walk you to the village. I need to get Dad's magazine."

They walked down the drive. Their feet crunching the gravel seemed to dominate the silence, with a few birds calling to each other. If he did leave Matthew, he didn't want him to be public enemy number one in the village. James held a lot of sway in the small community.

"Sorry he got the dig in about you three. He's still my father, I guess."

James chuckled. "I would have been worried if he hadn't."

"How is it all going?"

James kicked a larger stone into the flower bed. "Between the three of us, it's going perfectly. I've never known so much love. Ed and I rattled along for years and I had no idea what we were missing out on. Then Arthur came and opened us up to the world."

"Sounds perfect."

"It does, doesn't it? Downside is the whole bloody village feel like they have a stake in us. Some of the questions I've been asked are incredible."

Will could just imagine.

"It's like every pair of eyes are on us. Arthur and I had a spat the other day. Nothing major — he wanted to drive my car and I don't let anyone drive that baby. I don't care how in love with them I am. Seems someone saw us in the car park of The King's. I hadn't even got to Harrogate when our Liz was on the phone asking why we'd split up."

That side of Napthwaite gave Will nightmares.

They were on the road now and walking up to the green. The village looked so picturesque. People often visited here and desperately wanted to retire here. They never saw the darker undertone.

"How are you going to handle it?" Will asked.

"Oh, I'm used to it. Things will die down. I remember when our Liz came home from her travels, pregnant and on her own. Mum thought the village would never forgive her. Things sorted themselves out."

"I hate that people think they are some higher order and yes, that includes my father."

They were at the green now.

James glanced over at The King's. "At least I have that place. I guess none of us want to let our fathers down, no matter how hard it can be. Hey, that reminds me, I need your help."

Will sat on the edge of the bridge. "Sure thing."

"I don't suppose you know any chefs in the area? The food at my place is pretty shit and this is something the village have made clear they will not forgive for much longer. Arthur has been nagging like mad at me to just get someone in."

An idea started to form in Will's mind. "Are you just after someone to make the usual crap?"

James perched next to him. They were both facing the pub now. "Nah. I can't make a living from local trade only. I want to reinvent the place as a gastropub. It's a good opportunity for someone. I'll give them free rein in the kitchen and they can put their name to it. I don't know fuck all about food and Becky heats the scampi until they're like bloody bullets."

"And they can put their name on it?" Will asked.

"Yeah. A place in Brockle did that. A young lad got on that programme where they compete to serve the queen. People come from all over. The landlord rubbed my nose in it at the Brewers Ball the other week."

Will turned to James. "I'd love to do it."

James frowned. "You have a job in London. Your dad said you'll be taking over soon."

Will shook his head. "Dad has an overactive imagination. My boss is an arsehole and won't be going anywhere soon. Besides, I think I'm done with London life. I just don't know if I'm ready for Napthwaite again. I need to buy myself some thinking time."

They sat for a second, letting it sink in before James got up and stuck his hand out.

"Tell you what. How about you set us up? Get me a new menu sorted out and if you still feel the same way, then you're hired."

Will took his hand and shook it. He had just made a huge decision and it felt like the most natural thing in the world. He watched James walk off towards the pub. "Fucking hell," he said to himself before setting off to Brockbank's.

Chapter Fifteen

Wednesday night came around and Hardeep and Will were entwined on Andrew's couch. Andrew lay on the floor with his head against the sofa. Hardeep ran his hands through Andrew's hair.

"Take the bun out," he said.

Andrew moved his head. "No chance. You'll laugh."

"We won't," Will said.

Andrew sighed and fiddled with the band that held his hair firmly in place. Shaking his blond locks free, he turned around. He hardly ever had his hair down except when he went to sleep. He loved his long hair, but it did get in the way.

"Wow. Who is this Viking we have before us?" Will cried out.

"I knew you'd take the piss."

"Come here," Hardeep said, holding his arm out for Andrew.

Andrew crawled up onto the sofa, his big frame squashing the other two as he found his way underneath Hardeep. Wrapping his arms around him in a bear hug, he licked his neck, making him squirm.

"Vikings took what they wanted," he said. "I stake my claim on you two. Now you have to do what I say."

Will leapt off the sofa as Hardeep struggled to get free. "Don't just abandon me to this pillager," he managed.

Will pawed at Andrew's shorts. "Hey, what are you doing? That isn't playing fair."

He and Hardeep fell onto the floor, with Will on top of them, and they rolled around, laughing. Eventually Andrew got on top and looked down at the two men below him. They were so gorgeous in totally different ways that his cock started to wake up.

"I conquer."

Will held his hands up in mock protest. "Okay, okay. We concede. Do your worst, Mr Viking."

Andrew shook his mane so it stuck out everywhere. "I shall choose you first, Johnstone, before you run off to the capital."

"Ah."

Andrew frowned at Hardeep and flopped down on the floor next to him. "*Ah*? That sounds ominous. Don't tell us you're going back tomorrow?"

Hardeep sat up, his face a picture of concern. "Will?"

Will crawled up onto the sofa so that he faced them. Andrew protectively put his hand on Hardeep's leg. "So something happened this week and I've taken a bit of a leap of faith."

What could he have done?

"James Durkin came round to the house to talk to Dad about the parish council. They are advising that he needs to stand down. It's fair enough. He can hardly make himself a meal at the moment—he doesn't need the stress of all that on top."

Hardeep nodded. "Seems a good idea. Must have been hard for your dad, though."

"You wouldn't believe the upset it's caused, but I can get him on track."

Andrew admired Will for the way he had risen to the occasion over his father's illness. It was common knowledge that they hadn't had the easiest of relationships over the years and to have such a homophobe for a father must have been hell growing up. "And what's the big announcement then?" Surely Matthew Johnstone wasn't upping sticks and going to live in London.

"James mentioned that he wants someone to set up the pub as a proper food destination."

"About time," Hardeep declared. "When Mum did the curry night, everyone said it was nice to eat decent food in The King's."

"I like a challenge."

"You?" Hardeep and Andrew said at the same time.

"Me," Will confirmed.

Andrew didn't know what to think. His heart soared to think that Will would be staying in the village.

"Wow," Hardeep said. "That's brilliant news. So you're staying here?"

Will hugged a cushion. "For the time being. I've been freaking out ever since I said it. I haven't told Dad yet."

Andrew couldn't get his head around this huge decision Will had just made. "Are you sure? I thought you hated it around here."

"I feel it's where I need to be right now. Anton is trying to get me to go back and I'm not ready. I'm just sorting the menu out, then I've got the chance to go to New York with a friend. It feels like the universe is telling me to shake things up."

He got up off the sofa. "I'm nipping to the loo. A glass of wine would be nice on my return."

Andrew stood too. "I thought I was supposed to be the one demanding things." He went into the kitchen. Will's feet could be heard overhead. He reached into the fridge and produced a decent bottle of rose he'd been saving for them coming over.

"You're not having a freak-out, are you?" Hardeep said behind him, making him jump.

"Bloody hell, Kaur. You gave me a start."

Hardeep leant towards him. "Well?"

"A freak-out?"

Hardeep ran his hands around his waist. "He's doing this for his dad, you know. It's not some declaration of love that makes you sling us out again."

He had been so out of order the other night and had probably ruined one of the most special nights in Hardeep's life with his nonsense. "I'm sorry, Hardeep. I've got baggage but not that much."

Hardeep kissed him. "He needs us, you know. Whatever 'us' is. So do I, for that matter."

Andrew hadn't really thought about it. He'd had fun the other night and did enjoy the messaging and having people to check in with. But an "*us*"? That hadn't been in his game plan.

"You're thinking," Hardeep said.

They walked into the lounge and sat on each end of the couch.

"Not so much. I guess I hadn't really thought about things."

"Not much." Lisa's words were ringing in his ears. He wouldn't screw this up again. Even if they were only friends, they needed him, and he had to step up.

Will came into the lounge and sat in between them. "Have I shocked you?" he asked, accepting a glass from Andrew.

"You have a bit," Andrew said. "I thought you'd be in London as soon as you could."

"How can I leave him? I would just spend all the time worrying. I think London is done now. I don't know what the future holds. Dad still needs me and this opportunity came, so I thought, fuck it."

Hardeep raised his glass. "Fuck it."

Andrew slowly raised his, too. "Fuck it."

They sat in a silent row, sipping their wine. The mood needed lifting and Andrew decided it fell to him. "Talking of fucking it…wasn't there some talk of doing whatever I said?"

Will had a glint in his eye. "I remember something along those lines."

Andrew stood, stretching his tall frame. "Then get yourselves up those stairs. I've plans."

Will glanced at Hardeep. "I guess we'll have to."

Poor Hardeep looked like he was about to go to the executioner again. Will had told Andrew what he'd promised Hardeep when they'd parted the other night. He held his hand out for Hardeep and pulled him up off the sofa. He ran his hand around the small of his back, kissing him. "No need for that face," he murmured. "It's us, isn't it?"

Hardeep nodded. "It's us."

Andrew led the two men up the stairs into the bedroom. He remembered how he'd practically thrown them out last time they were in here and hoped they wouldn't be too preoccupied by it. He had some ground to make up and vowed to take on the responsibility. Once in the room, he pulled his T-shirt over his head and shook his hair out again.

"Should we be worried about this new alter ego?" Will said, unbuttoning his shirt.

"Time will tell," Andrew said, grabbing him by the waist and planting a kiss on his neck. He moved from Will to Hardeep, wrapping his arms around him and kissing him deeply. "Come on, I've been waiting for this for days," he said.

He threw the rest of his clothes off. His cock was already semi-hard and watching the other two getting naked would get it fully there. Lying down on the bed, he stroked himself as he watched.

Hardeep had got down to his boxers and made no attempt to hide his arousal. They soon fell to the floor, and he got onto the bed, slotting into Andrew's open arm.

Will, clearly not one to be left out, threw his clothes off and snuggled into his other side.

"This is more like it," Andrew said, kissing each one of the forehead.

Hardeep reached down and massaged his cock. Andrew closed his eyes for a second, luxuriating in the touch. He gently moved his hips in time. Feeling Will's lips on his, he returned the kiss, their tongues meeting each other. Then he turned and kissed Hardeep.

He couldn't hold his passion much longer. The heat from their bodies made him want them more than he'd wanted anything. Hardeep crawled on top of him, straddling him and kissing him hard.

Will disappeared down the end of the bed. Andrew broke the kiss to look over Hardeep's shoulder. Will winked at him and kissed Hardeep between the shoulder blades. Andrew pulled Hardeep closer to him, bending him over slightly while Will planted kisses down his spine.

When Andrew could see where he was headed, he whispered to Hardeep, "Just go with it."

"What the...?"

Andrew moved his head to the side to see Will delve his mouth between Hardeep's cheeks.

"Oh my God," Hardeep cried out.

"Okay?" Andrew said.

Hardeep managed a nod. Andrew ran his hands over his shoulders and brought him in for a kiss. Will eventually came up for air and moved up the bed, kissing Hardeep then Andrew.

"That was incredible," Hardeep sighed.

Andrew wriggled out from under Hardeep and moved around the bed. "Get on your hands and knees," he instructed Will.

Will did what he said, and Andrew buried his face in his ass. Will let out a moan. Hardeep, who seemed to be building in confidence, positioned himself so Will could suck his wet cock, which he did greedily.

Andrew ran his tongue up and down Will's arse, biting at the cheeks as he went. Will tensed when he hit the mark. Andrew wanted him so much. He ran his finger across Will's tight hole while massaging his cock with the other hand. He broke to reach into the bedside cabinet where he found condoms and lube.

Covering Will's hole with slick, he saw Hardeep watching him intently. "Come here," Andrew murmured.

Hardeep moved round the bed, watching Andrew who slid his finger in and out of Will's hole. Will moaned and leant right down, giving them all the access they needed.

Andrew got a condom out of the wrapper but instead of putting it on his cock, he rolled it over Hardeep's. Hardeep gulped, but Andrew nodded. Hardeep positioned himself so the end of his cock pushed on Will's hole. Andrew stood behind him, his own cock pressing against Hardeep's arse and his hands wrapped around him.

"Slowly," he murmured in Hardeep's ear. He gently pressed his body onto Hardeep's hips, causing Hardeep's cock to slide slowly into Will.

Hardeep leant his head back and Andrew kissed his neck. Will moaned into a pillow as Hardeep's hard cock reached its base.

"Now hold it for a second," Andrew said, moving his hands up Hardeep's body. "Let him get used to it."

Will lifted his head up. "Fuck me."

Andrew laid a guiding hand on Hardeep's arse. He pushed until Hardeep was pumping Will's hole. "Oh, fuck this feels good," Hardeep said.

"I'll bloody say," Will gasped.

Andrew moved away, watching Hardeep fuck Will like a pro. His own cock needed attention, but all in good time. The floorshow in front of him was one of the horniest things he'd ever seen.

Hardeep was fucking Will intensely.

"Come for me, Hardeep, please," Will moaned.

"You sure?"

"For now, come on."

Sweat fell from Hardeep's forehead onto Will's back as he pounded him. Suddenly he let out a yell and arched his body. "Oh God yeah."

His body still shaking, Hardeep pulled out. Andrew had already rolled a condom onto his own cock. He flipped Will over and put his legs on his shoulders. Spreading his own legs for stability, he pushed the tip of his cock where Hardeep had just been.

Will opened his eyes. Andrew was hung and many a guy hadn't been able to take him. He desperately hoped this wouldn't be the case tonight, because he wanted to fuck Will badly.

Will nodded and Andrew slowly slid inside. Will gripped the duvet cover with his hands, panting as he pushed right up to the base. He could see Hardeep watching him from the side, and so leant across and kissed him. Hardeep ran his hands through his hair.

Slowly Andrew bucked his hips. With each movement, Will let out a cry, but one of passion.

"More," he demanded.

Andrew picked up the speed a little.

"More," Will said again. "I need it."

Andrew leant forward so Will's knees were up round his ears. He kissed him and moved his hips faster while their tongues danced together. As he fucked Will, he felt breath on his arse and suddenly Hardeep's tongue lapped at his hole. Moving away from the kiss, Andrew cried out, "Oh fuck yeah."

He positioned so Hardeep could get full access while Andrew carried on fucking Will. Will's body was covered in sweat. Andrew couldn't last much longer and reached down to Will's cock.

"I'll come," he said.

"Good."

In no time Will let out a cry. Andrew was just behind him and his body contorted with pleasure as he came.

Once they'd cleaned themselves up and were in one another's arms on the bed, Andrew couldn't have felt more bliss.

"You're a quick learner, Kaur," Andrew said, kissing him.

"Well at risk of being flung out on my ear, I'm really fucking happy right now."

Andrew took the barb in good spirits. "I'm really fucking happy too," he agreed.

Chapter Sixteen

"Turn that music down. I won't tell you again."

Mohinder banged on the ceiling of the shop with her broom handle. Hardeep shook his head.

"Give her a break, Mum."

"She's frightening the customers away."

Hardeep took in the empty shop. The struggle to get customers seemed to get harder each year. He didn't think Satinder playing her boybands would have much impact. "Your hollering is going to draw them in, is it?"

The music stopped.

"Thank goodness for that," Mohinder said, resuming her dusting.

The two women in his life were squaring up to each other more and more. Hardeep hated being caught in the middle. A few years ago, they'd been inseparable. Now they felt like two boxers with him in the middle.

"What were you banging on the floor for?" Satinder stood at the bottom of the stairs that led up to their flat.

"You know very well, young lady," muttered Mohinder.

Satinder gave him a glare. "Am I not allowed to play music now?"

"Maybe you could wear those headphones I got you for your birthday?" Hardeep leapt in before his mother could stoke the flames.

"I'm going out anyway," she said.

"You should be doing your schoolwork," Mohinder said.

Satinder sighed.

"Have you done your work?" he asked.

"Yes, I've done it. Do you want to check it?"

"Satinder, there's no need for the tone," he chided.

With another exceptionally dramatic sigh, she turned to walk away.

"Just a minute," Hardeep said. "What time will you be home?"

Satinder stopped in her tracks and turned around. "Is nine okay?"

Behind him, Mohinder made a disapproving noise.

"Nine o'clock? On a school night? Where are you going?" he asked, ignoring his mother.

Satinder shifted uneasily.

"Satinder. Where are you going?"

"Me and Kelly are getting the bus into Holton. Some friends are meeting up in the park."

Mohinder couldn't bear to be out of the conversation anymore and pushed past Hardeep. "Drinking in the park, I bet."

"Yes, and drugs and boys," Satinder shouted in retaliation at her grandmother.

Hardeep held his hand up. "Stop. Both of you. Satinder, don't speak to your grandmother like that. And, Mother, leave my daughter to me. Go on."

Still grumbling under her breath, Mohinder resumed her dusting. Hardeep pulled a ten-pound note out of his pocket. "Get some chips or something."

Satinder took the note. "You always take her side then give me money."

Without waiting for a reply, she turned on her heel and walked out of the flat. Beeb barked at the top of the stairs.

"Of course she wouldn't take her dog to the bloody park," Hardeep said.

Mohinder turned around to say something.

"Don't say a word. Honestly, I've had enough."

The day dragged on like that. Mohinder would get a dig in whenever she could until eventually she went off to Brockbank's for a cup of tea. No doubt Mrs Turnbull would be hot on her heels. She spent most of the afternoon there before silently returning upstairs with no offer of helping him. At last, five o'clock came and he went out to put the shutters down.

"Another day done?"

He turned around to see Liz Poole's son. "Hello, Dean. How are you doing?"

Dean shook his head. "Getting some peace. Mum has got wind that Matthew Johnstone is stepping down from the parish council. Guess who she thinks should replace him."

Hardeep cast his mind to the planning feud of a few weeks ago. Liz had been hellbent on building an awful modern extension to her shop. It had taken her own brother to turn on her as parish council chair to stop it. He didn't much fancy his chances if she got her feet under the table.

"There may be trouble ahead," he sang.

Dean gave him a knowing look. "There's always trouble when my mother's around."

"I know that feeling."

Once he'd shut up the shop, he went up to the flat. Mohinder was knitting and staring out of the window at the street below.

"I haven't made anything for dinner," she said. The ice hadn't thawed.

Hardeep made himself a cheese sandwich. His mother cast another disapproving glare. "I don't know why you're sore with me," Hardeep said between bites.

Mohinder put her knitting down. "I just want her to be a decent person, Hardeep."

Hardeep sat on the sofa. Beneath the battle-axe exterior, she had always been there for him. He hated this shift in their relationship. "I know you do, Mum. But times are different than when you were bringing us up. You have to give her a bit of freedom. She's fifteen. You were married at her age."

She patted him on the knee. "And look what that brought me. Maybe you're right. I will try."

Beeb sat patiently next to Hardeep, never once taking his eyes from the sandwich.

"There we go," he said, feeding him a titbit he'd saved.

"That dog will get fat," Mohinder sniffed.

Hardeep got up from the sofa and kissed his mother on the cheek.

"What is that for?"

"Because you're my mother. Right come on, Beeb. Let's take you out, work that tiny piece of cheese off."

Mohinder playfully slapped him on the leg. "You're not too old for a smack either."

"I won't be too long, Mum. I feel like a big walk though. It's a beautiful night."

Mohinder resumed her knitting. "I don't know why you've suddenly started walking at night. Don't you get enough in the day?"

Hardeep put the lead onto Beeb. "I like taking my little co-pilot here."

He needed to meet Will in ten minutes. Grabbing his keys, he half ran down the stairs and out onto Queen Street. Poor little Beeb had to trot to keep up with him.

Will and Titus were at the green.

"Hello, handsome," Will said quietly.

Instinctively Hardeep looked around.

"Relax," Will soothed. "Come on."

They made their way up the familiar track to Andrew's. He had been saying he would show them the plantation he'd been working on. The village were really behind this project, and he complained that he'd shown nearly everyone round but them.

When they got there, they couldn't find him anywhere.

"Andrew," Will shouted.

Sally pushed her way through the door at the bottom of the stairs.

"Hello, girl," Hardeep said, bending down to stroke her.

She solemnly presented a toy each to Beeb and Titus, and all three dogs settled on the rug for a communal destruction session.

"They're happy then," Will said.

"Where is he?"

Will pointed to the ceiling. "One guess."

Laughing like schoolchildren, they made their way upstairs. They burst through the bedroom door and there lay a naked Andrew.

"Took you long enough."

"I guess we're not going to the woods then," Hardeep said.

Andrew stroked his rapidly hardening cock. "Enough wood here."

Will put his head in his hands. "Corny."

Andrew pouted. "Shut up and get your kit off."

* * * *

A couple of hours later, they lay entwined on the bed. The summer breeze drifted in through the window, drying the sweat on their bodies. The dogs had obviously sensed stillness and made their way up to the room. Sally had staked her claim at the foot of the bed, and Titus and Beeb lay on the floor.

Hardeep could see the hilltops out of the window. He envied Andrew living on the edge of everything. It could get overwhelming in the middle of the village.

"I can't stay too long," Will murmured, half dozing. "Dad is upset since he had to retire from the council."

Hardeep thought about his conversation with Dean. "You know who's a dead cert to replace him?"

Will and Andrew both shook their heads.

"Liz Poole."

"No way will anyone vote for her," Andrew said. "She's been a right sod this year."

Neither of these two had any clue how villages worked. "They won't have to if she doesn't have anyone against her."

They lay in silence for a second. Hardeep had hated watching the village divide when Liz had started her campaign against Arthur. Things seemed to be on the level there now but who would be her next target?

"You should stand," Will announced, tapping Andrew on the chest.

"Me? Don't be ridiculous."

"Why not? Everyone loves your project. You're perfect."

"Will's right," Hardeep said. "A handsome man with a dog? You'd be a natural."

They all burst into laughter. Sally raised her head to check on them.

"I think there's more to it than that," Andrew said.

"Not really. Dad just went to meetings and moaned. You can do that."

"Hey, you," Andrew said, kissing him.

"You'd get my vote," Hardeep told him. He got a kiss in return.

Andrew settled on the pillow. "Maybe I'll look into it."

They lay there for a while longer. It would have been so perfect if it hadn't been for the niggling seed of doubt that had started to grow in the back of Hardeep's mind. He couldn't ignore it any longer. "Guys," he said.

Will sat up. He shot a concerned glance at Andrew.

"This doesn't sound good," Andrew said.

Hardeep took a second. "This is amazing. Truly it is. But…"

"There's always a but," Will said.

"Please let me speak," Hardeep replied. "But things aren't going well at home. Mum and Sat are at each other's throat's morning, noon and night. The shop is struggling. All I care about is telling lies and finding my way to this bed. I don't know…"

Will reached across Andrew's body and took Hardeep's hand. "What are you saying?"

The emotion bubbled away in Hardeep like a dormant volcano. He hadn't even thought about starting this conversation, but his worries weren't going away. "I'm not saying anything. I just don't know if I can fit everything together."

Andrew put his big hand over the two of theirs and pressed them onto his chest.

"It doesn't have to fit together. You're overthinking it. This can only ever be fun, so let's not get carried away."

"Why do you do this?" Will asked.

Andrew turned around. Hardeep had detected a tone in Will's voice, and he hoped he hadn't started something.

"Do what?" Andrew asked.

"Always put this down to a one-night stand that went on a bit longer?" Will answered.

Andrew sat still for a second. Then he grabbed a pillow, threw it to the foot of the bed and lay down facing them. "I think the time has come to be honest with you."

Hardeep plumped up the remaining pillows. He and Will cuddled together. Will reached forward and stroked Andrew's foot.

"I didn't just come here to plant a load of new trees, "Andrew started. "I came to escape."

Hardeep didn't dare look at Will. The atmosphere in the room had gone very serious. Beeb didn't pick up on that and yapped on the floor. He leant down and scooped him up, cuddling him against his bare chest. "Sorry. He has no decorum."

"What were you escaping from?" Will asked.

"My ex, Neil. He is a bastard and a drunk." Andrew lifted his long hair up to reveal a scar on his neck. "That was from a broken wine bottle when I wouldn't let him change the channel on the TV."

They both looked at him, horrified. He lifted his thigh and pointed to the scar that Hardeep had run his tongue along only minutes before. "He went for me with a kitchen knife on Christmas day when I suggested he slow down the drinking."

Hardeep had assumed he got scars in his line of work. He had never thought someone would have been responsible. "Andrew, that is awful. How long were you with him for?" he asked.

"Four years. You'd think I would have got out sooner but..."

"You loved him," Will said with a bitter smile.

Andrew nodded. "I should have known better, but I thought I could change him. I tried everything."

Hardeep ran his hand up Andrew's leg. He wanted to comfort him as best he could. "What happened?"

"One night he smashed me over the head with a wine bottle. I pushed him off me and he fell backwards. I didn't do any damage, but he called the police and they hauled me off. I spent a night in the cells. I did a lot of thinking in there, I can tell you."

The silence in the room was palpable.

"The next morning, they questioned me, and it all came out. All of a sudden, I went from criminal to victim. To cut a long story short, I got a court order out on him. He's not allowed to come near me. I didn't want to leave it at that, so I did a runner. It's not so far from Sheffield but far enough."

Hardeep put Beeb down on the floor and crawled up to Andrew. He kissed him on the lips. "You are brave. Thank you for telling us."

Will followed suit. "We won't hurt you. That you can be sure of."

"Maybe. Maybe not. But do me a favour. Let's not make this out to be anything else. I can't take any more stress."

Will and Andrew started to kiss. Hardeep watched them, feeling his cock responding.

Andrew might not want this to be anything more than fun and to these two who had lived a worldly life, they probably found it easy to keep it in a box. But Hardeep had started to develop feelings for both of them.

He had no idea if he could control them. But he would have to.

Because if he didn't, he could lose everything.

Chapter Seventeen

The posters were up everywhere. Lisa had sent them to her printer supplier and they were great. A picture of him and Sally in the woods accompanied them. He looked so wholesome that he hardly recognised himself. He wondered what the village would say if they found out he was banging the postman and the previous councillor's son. Liz would no doubt be all over that.

Her posters were homemade and lame in comparison. Hardeep had told him that most people he spoke to were supporting Andrew. They didn't want two siblings on the council and certainly didn't want Liz's space-age extension.

When Hardeep had suggested he stand, he had agreed without really thinking about it. Once he'd got Lisa onto the case, he might as well have been running for parliament. Before things got completely out of hand, he had come to the pub. James and Becky were behind the bar.

"Hello there," James said with his trademark grin.

"Pint?" Becky added.

"Why not?" Andrew replied.

Becky pulled the pint while Sally sat next to him patiently. James took the not very subtle hint and lifted the lid on a jar. "Don't suppose the lady would care for a biscuit or two?"

"I'm sure she would."

James grabbed a handful of biscuits and came around the bar. He leant down and fed them to the grateful Sally, who allowed him to scratch behind her ears.

"Can I have a word?" Andrew said, handing Becky a five-pound note.

"Course you can."

James beckoned him over to a table. They sat and Andrew took a big gulp of his lager. For the first six months after he'd left Neil, he hadn't touched a drop. But with Lisa coming into his life and him playing for the rugby team, he'd realised he could handle his drink. Now he enjoyed it, but he rarely got drunk. Usually Lisa would be the one to break that resolution.

"I bet I can guess what this is about," James said.

"I don't want any trouble. What has Liz got to say?"

Becky burst out laughing.

"That's enough from you, thank you," James said with a glint in his eye. "I won't lie to you. She's not impressed. My sister likes things her way. She's had enough compromising this year to last her a lifetime."

Andrew hadn't dared go into her shop since it had been announced a week ago. He had sent Hardeep in to get him some essentials before their Wednesday night meet-up. "And what about you?"

"I'm not in the market for another feud with her, but as chair, I'm neutral. Whoever wins will be welcomed. No hard feelings whatsoever."

"You've got my vote," Becky piped up.

James grabbed a sachet of ketchup from the table and threw it at her. "Don't you have some cleaning to do?"

A group of walkers came in through the door, and Becky set about serving them. Andrew heard voices coming from the back, and James' other partner, Arthur, came into the bar followed by Will. It took all his power not to pull Will into a bear hug.

"What have we here?" Arthur said, sitting on the chair next to James. "Two handsome men plotting, by the looks of it."

Will slid onto the banquette next to Andrew. He sat far closer than he needed to, and Andrew revelled in their bodies touching.

"Andrew was just asking if I minded him standing for the council," James said.

Arthur raised an eyebrow. "Anyone who can give Liz a run for her money is all right in my books."

James put his arm around his shoulder. "Keep that opinion to yourself, please. We're still on shaky ground."

Arthur made a face.

"What are you doing here?" Andrew asked Will.

"I've made a start revolutionising the food offering. No offence, but it's not hard."

James shook his head. "Is it a prerequisite for working here that you have to give me grief at every possible opportunity? Don't tell me you and Becky have formed some kind of union."

"Hey, I've just had a thought," Will said. "Why don't we do a meet the candidate night? I could cater and we could get some local journalists in. I bet Lisa knows the right people."

James held his hands up. "Don't even think about having it here."

"Wimp," Arthur said, putting his hand on James' knee.

"We'll have it at the village hall then," Will said, clearly on a roll.

"It might not be a bad idea," Arthur agreed. "You're still a newcomer in these parts. People will want to know what you believe in."

Andrew took a swig of his drink and thought about it. "Are you sure, Will?"

"Of course. A few canapes are easy enough. Lisa can bring some booze. Happy days."

Some more walkers came into the pub.

"I'd better give Becky a hand," James said, getting up and going behind the bar.

Arthur's face grew serious. "Tread carefully with Liz. She's trouble. I nearly lost everything thanks to her. Don't get me wrong—we're working on things, but only because I love James so much."

Will turned to Andrew. "I'm done here. How about we have a planning session at yours then head off to Holton for supplies?"

Andrew drained his pint. "You're on."

* * * *

Preparations for the event filled his week. Hardeep agreed to slip a flier into people's post, and Lisa had come up with some crates of wine. She also threw in some new beers she wanted to trial. Andrew suspected he shouldn't really be promoting alcohol but he couldn't be bothered arguing with her.

As he walked into the village hall, the nerves jangled inside him. He had a table at the top of the room covered in bunting. He would sit there and receive his visitors. Everyone else would mill around, being served by a couple of Lisa's brewery men who had agreed to some extra hours.

The canapes that Will had made gave it a classy vibe. He doubted Liz would stretch to a bargain packet of biscuits. He and Hardeep stood across the room with a bottle of beer each.

"Not bad, Lisa," Will said, holding the bottle up.

Lisa gave him a weak smile. "Forgive me if I don't use that review on the marketing blurb."

Andrew came over to them and Will handed him a bottle. "One for the nerves?"

Gratefully he swigged it down. "I'm bloody terrified."

The hall had started to fill up. Mohinder and Satinder came over to the three of them. Mohinder looked her son up and down.

"The amount of time you three spend together, you may as well get married to them," she said. "People will start to talk."

"Gran," Satinder exclaimed. "What is the matter with you? Sorry about her."

"Hello, Mrs Kaur," Will said, putting on his best virtuous face. "Hello, Satinder."

"Hello, William," Mohinder said, ignoring her granddaughter. "How's your father?"

"Every day is victory."

They stood awkwardly as the conversation ran aground. Andrew could see on Hardeep's face his total discomfort having his mother next to his two lovers.

For the umpteenth time, Andrew checked his pocket for his speech. He had spent ages writing it and kept panicking that he had left it somewhere. Public speaking was one thing—freestyling did not appeal. Before he could make a move to the podium, everyone looked at the door and gasped.

Matthew Johnstone stood there and stared at Will, fury written all over his face. "How could you do this to me?"

Will resembled a teenager caught drinking behind the bus shed. "Dad, listen…"

"Don't you *Dad* me. It's bad enough that I have the humiliation of standing down. Now you're helping my replacement? Or did you buy these in Poole's?" He held up a mini bruschetta as though it were key evidence at a murder trial.

"Andrew is my friend. I'm just—"

Matthew threw the offending canape at his son and turned on his heel to stalk out of the village hall.

Will sighed. "I'd better go after him."

Andrew nodded. He had to stop himself kissing Will on the cheek. It would have been the most natural thing in the world. He exchanged a glance with Hardeep instead.

"We don't need any drama tonight," Lisa said, coming over. Since she'd assumed the role of campaign manager, she had tried to control everything. Andrew quite happily let her. He had no idea what to do and had started to think this whole foray into politics more trouble than it was worth.

"Come on, you. The journos want a picture and some quotes. No rest for a budding politician."

She half-dragged him over to the other side of the room where a woman in a twin set and pearls and a man in jeans and faded Led Zeppelin T-shirt waited for him. It didn't look like he would be worrying Fleet Street any time soon.

The woman thrust her hand out. "Philippa Gibbons of the *Holton Examiner*. I wondered if I could ask, what prompted you to stand?"

"Oh, well, I believe in this village. They have been very good to me and I'm keen to give as much back as I can."

She looked impressed as she made notes in a floral notebook. The man to Andrew's right looked totally uninterested.

"Spike will need some pictures. Perhaps after your speech. I'm sure you're nervous. What are your key concerns for the village?"

He had rehearsed this. "I want the feel of the village to be protected. It is a beautiful place for locals and visitors alike."

A wry smile crept on her face. "So, no modern extensions then?"

Andrew matched her grin. "I couldn't possibly comment."

Lisa seemed keen to wrap this up. It was nearly seven and people had started to fidget. "Can we finish this later when you do the photos? Andrew…Mr Norris has a speech to give."

The butterflies threatened to overpower him as he made his way to the stage. Lisa darted in front of him and checked the microphone like some crazed roadie. "All good," she said.

He tried to return it but thought he could be sick at any minute. This had seemed a great idea in the post-coital fuzz. It felt very different now as dozens of pairs of eyes stared expectedly at him.

"Ladies and gentlemen. Thank you for coming today —"

Before he could get any further, the doors banged open and a short but very attractive woman stood in the doorway.

By the gasps from some of the older locals, she wasn't a stranger to everyone.

"Satinder? Is that you?" the woman said.

Satinder looked uncertainly to her father, who seemed transfixed. Mohinder let out a gasp and clutched him. The woman dashed over to them and grabbed Satinder into a hug. Hardeep hadn't moved a muscle as she smirked at him over the shoulder of his daughter.

"What's the matter? Haven't you got anything to say to your own wife?"

Chapter Eighteen

When Will left the village hall, he saw his father walking down Queen Street. It broke his heart to see him shuffling down the road, the anger still evident but his body letting him down.

Will's first instinct was to catch up with him, but he held back. He toyed with returning to the Hall, but Mrs Turnbull had taken in the whole argument, and she'd report to Matthew that Will hadn't been able to stay away.

Andrew would be fine without him. He had done his bit. Instead he turned and walked out of the village. The hubbub of the hall soon faded away as he walked down the lane past Mrs Carrington's cottage.

He sat on the bridge where he used to play Pooh Sticks with his mother. The familiar ache of loss throbbed in his heart. It had been decades since he'd seen her beautiful smile. Being surrounded by places he had been to with her had started to make his resolve crumble. He'd found it easy to compartmentalise her in his life in London. There she was nothing more than a photo in a frame. Here he couldn't move for memories of her.

She had always been able to handle Matthew and his moods. If he was being gruff, she would send Will out to play. Eventually his parents would emerge from Matthew's study calm, and Matthew would start up a game with him.

She had been the glue that held them together.

"Penny for them?" Michael Fleming came and perched on the end of the bridge.

"Hi," Will said.

"I saw you have a bit of a run-in with your dad. Are you okay?"

Will nodded even though he wasn't fully sure it was true.

"I hear you're working at The King's," Michael said.

"Yeah. It's only a bit of consulting. I wanted to buy myself some thinking time. I reckon New York is the end destination."

Michael whistled. "Sounds fancy. Have you told your old boss?"

Will shook his head.

"What's stopping you?"

"I don't know. The finality of it all. It's a big step."

"Sounds like you've already made the decision in your head. Dragging it out won't do any good."

"You know what you're right. I'm going to ring him right now."

"No time like the present, I guess. Well, I'll leave you to it. There's a pint with your name on if you need it."

"Thanks."

Michael walked off towards the village and, with butterflies raging, Will dialled the number.

"You're on unpaid leave now, you know."

"Hello to you too, Anton. My father is getting better every day, thanks for asking."

"If you're ringing to ask for another month, you can fuck off. We're run off our feet here."

Will knew he should feel anger but instead an overwhelming sadness came over him. That he had spent so long waiting for Anton to be a decent person made him feel a bit of a fool.

"Actually, I'm not coming back. Ever. So you'd better stick your job up your arse, Anton."

The silence on the other end only made his spirits soar higher. He watched the stream babbling past while Anton got himself together.

"How dare you?"

"Easy. You've treated me like shit for the best part of ten years. I'm telling you to go fuck yourself. I would have thought that would be straightforward. Even for you."

"I will blacklist you in every restaurant in London, you jumped-up little twat."

He couldn't have planned this better if he'd tried. "Do your worst. I'm through with London anyway."

"I won't give you a reference."

"That's your choice. My new job will do when I finally move on."

"Your... What the fuck?"

Will took aim with his parting shot. "Oh, and as for that interview with HR. I've decided a letter is more appropriate. I always forget things when I'm put on the spot. I've made sure I captured everything. I know you hate me cutting corners. Bye, Anton."

Just as Anton started to let out yet another string of expletives, Will terminated the call. The elation overwhelmed him. He leant against the wall and thought about what he had just done. No doubt a waiter or two would cop it today, but Will couldn't think about that now. He had taken control and it felt good.

He set off home to field another argument with his father. Then he turned and stopped, going back to the bridge and snapping a twig off a tree. He threw it into the babbling stream and dashed across the bridge. He waited until it appeared and watched it float away into the distance.

"I love you, Mum."

He didn't fancy bumping into anyone at the Hall so he took the alleyway behind the shops. He couldn't see a soul. They must all still be at Andrew's party. That made him feel good. Andrew deserved a proper new start.

Once he got indoors, the radio was playing in the kitchen. Matthew didn't usually frequent that room, so Will put his head around the door. His father shuffled around the kitchen, struggling to make himself a drink. Will walked in and guided his father to the kitchen table.

"Tea?"

Matthew still had an angry face on. "I can do it."

"I'm not saying you can't, but I'd like to."

Matthew nodded.

Will let the silence reign while he made them a drink. They needed to get used to each other. If he approached things too quickly, it would turn into another argument. He didn't want that. Not this time. He put the cups down and sat at the opposite end of the table.

"Are we going to have a talk?" Matthew asked.

"Nope," Will said, blowing on his tea. "I'm going to say something and you're going to listen."

An astonished Matthew stared at his son. Will thought he could detect a hint of interest.

"Go on then."

"I am not being disloyal to you by helping Andrew. You aren't standing. I know it's hard to accept that your time at the council is over, but that isn't my doing. I can't let you take all your frustrations out on me, Dad. Especially not in public. Do you know how humiliating that was for me?"

Matthew shifted uncomfortably.

"I'm thirty-five years old. I'm a professional with a life in London—"

"You chose to come here. I didn't send for you."

Will ignored his interruption. "I came here because I love you."

This time Matthew stopped in his tracks. They hadn't said they loved each other for decades.

"I stay here because I'm finding that I like the old place. I shut the door on Napthwaite for so many years because it reminded me of Mum."

Matthew flinched.

"Dad, I have to be able to talk about my mother. You're the only person who knew her like I did."

"I know," Matthew said quietly.

"Talk to me, Dad. Tell me how you're feeling instead of taking it out on me."

Matthew ran his hands through his thinning white hair. "That's not how I do things, you know that."

Will got up and sat on the chair next to his father. He took his hand. Matthew tried to move away, but Will had far more strength and held him in place. "You have to start," he pleaded. "I'm going to level with you. I've just quit the restaurant for good. I've been coasting. I want to see it through at The King's for a few months, then give New York a try."

Matthew relaxed his hand and let Will's remain on top of it. "But you were going to open somewhere in London. All that is for nothing."

"Nothing is for nothing. Let's really try to get along, Dad. If you could just allow me to care for you, even just a little, it would be so much better for both of us. Whether you like it or not, you need me right now."

By asserting his independence, he had no intention of taking away all his father's power in the process. That would finish a man like Matthew Johnstone off.

"I suppose I don't mind you staying here while you're between jobs."

Only his father could turn this around so that he was doing him a favour. Will smiled. Victory came in all shapes and sizes and this was the best he could have hoped for.

"That's very good of you, Dad. Now, tea or coffee?"

Chapter Nineteen

"I never thought I'd win the fucking thing," Andrew proclaimed as they walked up the brow of the hill. They were racing through September, and October would bring the usual wet weather, so they wanted to get the dogs out onto the hills while they had the chance.

Beeb had long since given up walking and nestled in Hardeep's backpack. They were big hills for such little legs. Titus and Sally had no such qualms and were racing through the undergrowth after all the scents.

"Well, you have." Will laughed. "Must have been my canapes."

"Or the newspaper interview," Andrew added. "Did you know, Hardeep, your mother asked me to sign a copy?"

Hardeep seemed lost in thought. He had been distant ever since his ex-wife had turned up at the hall. They found a rock to sit on and Will got a flask out. It was still pretty warm for autumn, but as Will handed Andrew a mug of steaming coffee, he had to admit, he needed it.

"You still having grief?" Will asked Hardeep.

To Andrew's horror, Hardeep burst into tears. Will went to comfort him. Beeb, who had been released temporarily when they'd stopped, came fussing around his feet.

Hardeep pulled himself together. "I'm sorry, guys. We haven't met up for ages and I wanted today to be perfect, but she's turned everything upside down."

They hadn't met for a fortnight. Andrew had been preoccupied with his election duties, and Will had thrown himself into this menu at The King's. Andrew realised they hadn't done their duty by Hardeep and had left him to deal with this new situation on his own.

"Tell us about it," Andrew said, rubbing Hardeep's leg.

"Where to bloody begin? Satinder is over the moon that her mother has remembered she exists."

Will handed him a cup from his rucksack and filled it up with coffee. "Where is she staying?"

"Leeds for now. But she's been coming here every chance she gets. She's taken Sat shopping, to the cinema, a gig… What a wonderful mother, eh? I just nag her to pick her dirty socks up, do her homework and stop cheeking her gran."

"She must be doing all right cash-wise," Andrew pondered.

"Oh, she is. She has a new man. He owns a load of bars in Tenerife. That's where she's been all this time. Sat accused me of driving her away last night. I can just imagine all the shit she's filling her head with."

The wind rustled through the leaves and dislodged a branch which fell down behind them. Sally and Titus set off to investigate this occurrence. Beeb decided to bark from behind Hardeep's legs. He reached down and rubbed his ears, silencing him immediately.

"Can't you make it more formal?" Will asked.

Hardeep shook his head. "She's fifteen. She can make her own mind up. Me coming down heavy will just play into Bina's hands. She'll say I'm jealous. That's not the worst of it."

"Go on, "Andrew said.

"I overheard her on the phone to one of her mates the other night. She's planning on going to Tenerife to work in Uncle Wayne's bar for the summer. I will lose her."

The tears came again. This time Andrew and Will let them run their course.

"You won't lose her," Will soothed. "You're her dad and she loves you. But you can't blame her for being curious."

Andrew dug in his pocket and handed Hardeep a tissue which he dutifully blew his nose into.

"I get that, truly I do. But I know what she's like. It's all roses now, but when she gets bored, Sat will be so let down."

Will sighed. "That's the thing. You can't protect her from everything, no matter how much you want to. Some lessons in life she has to learn for herself. All you can do is be there for her if and when it all goes tits up."

As they had been talking, the clouds had darkened. The first spot of rain hit Andrew right between the eyes.

"Oh shit, it didn't forecast this," Andrew exclaimed. As an avid fan of the weather channel, he prided himself on knowing exactly what would be happening to the valley.

More drops of rain followed.

Will looked around. "Over there, quickly," he said, pointing to an old rundown stone building that had been built for shepherds to shelter in many years ago.

They grabbed their things and the dogs. Running across the fellside, the rain came in droves. Breathless, they made it to the hut still fairly dry.

Hardeep had picked Beeb up, but he squirmed to be released and trotted off to his bigger friends. They all curled up in the corner together. "Dogs aren't stupid," Hardeep said, watching them.

Andrew glanced out of the door. The shower didn't seem as if it would last very long. He turned to the other two, who were taking their wet coats off. "Maybe we should take a leaf out of their book."

Will and Hardeep glanced at each other.

Andrew threw his coat down on the floor. He took Will and Hardeep's and made a comfy space. Dropping to his knees in front of Hardeep, he reached across and started to undo his zip.

The anxiety that had been written all over Hardeep's face moments ago was replaced by a much more carnal look as Andrew set his cock free.

Andrew smiled as it hardened at his touch. He slowly massaged the cock, lightly licking the tip. Hardeep leant back, moaning. Will moved behind him and unbuttoned his shirt. The minute that he exposed Hardeep's hairy chest to the elements, Andrew took his whole cock in his mouth.

He glanced up to see Will kissing Hardeep's neck and playing with his nipples, something that they had discovered drove Hardeep crazy.

Andrew sucked on Hardeep's cock. His own hard cock pressing against the fabric confines of his boxers and canvas walking trousers. He reached down and flicked open the button and fly. Will moved around from Hardeep's body and crouched down. He pushed his hand into Andrew's trousers, making him tingle as he squeezed his dick.

Andrew groaned as he sucked greedily at Hardeep. Will pulled Andrew's cock out and bent to suck him.

Will's head bobbed up and down Andrew's rock-hard cock. Andrew cursed himself for not bringing a condom. He had grown to love fucking Will's tight arse.

Coming up for air, Will winked at him.

"Take your trousers off," Andrew instructed.

Will glanced out of the open door. "What if someone sees us?"

"Who the fuck is going to see us?" Andrew said, licking his lips. "Go on."

Will stood and dropped his trousers, soon followed by his boxers so they were at his ankles. Andrew sat up and pulled Will to him by his waist. He took his cock in his mouth, causing Will to cry out.

Hardeep kissed Will. Andrew swapped from one cock to the other and back again. His mouth watering each time he tasted them. He felt so horny, being responsible for both men's pleasure.

These two men were so handsome in such different ways.

"Come on me," he said, opening his shirt.

They both were tugging at their cocks as Andrew did the same.

Hardeep came first. Andrew moaned with pleasure as the hot liquid fell onto his chest. Will soon followed suit, his cum mingling with Hardeep's on Andrew's chest.

Andrew revelled in the feeling of his lovers' cum on him. He pulled at his own cock until he juddered to a powerful climax. Closing his eyes, he sank back on the coats to calm down.

"I bloody told you someone would see us," Will said.

Quick as a flash, Andrew opened his eyes to see two sheep peering in through the door. They all burst into laughter.

Andrew had been right—the shower hadn't lasted long. By the time they had cleaned themselves up, the sunshine poked through the clouds.

"Sorry I can't do anything tonight," Andrew said when they got to his garden gate.

"First day on the council?" Hardeep said. "A very important day indeed."

"Hey," Andrew said. He gave Hardeep a hug. "It will all work out, you know. Things always do."

There were tears in Hardeep's eyes. "Thank you."

Andrew gave Will a hug too. "We need a fuck soon. All of us."

The interlude in the old shelter had made him hornier than before. He watched Hardeep and Will walk down the path to the village. Will's trousers clung to his butt that was so irresistible. Andrew shook his head.

If only I didn't have the bloody council.

But he did and he wanted to make a good impression. He dashed into the house, where he put on a clean pair of jeans and a nicely ironed checked shirt. He didn't want to look too formal, but first impressions counted.

By the time he stood outside the village hall, his nerves were pretty bad. He reasoned with himself that he knew everyone on the council, so he had nothing to fear. He also suspected that most of the people in there would be relieved Liz Poole hadn't made it. He wandered in. As usual he had arrived fifteen minutes early and the only person in there was James.

"Wow, you're keen," James said.

Andrew walked up to the table. "Where should I sit?"

James beckoned to the seat next to him. "This was always Matthew's favourite place. You might as well have that one. You okay?"

"Yeah, bit nervous to tell you the truth."

"Nothing to be nervous about," James smiled. "Try coming in here when you've declared you're sleeping with two other men. Although you've replaced the only person who had a problem with it."

Andrew thought about Matthew collapsing at the village fete. It had only been two months ago, but it had set off a chain reaction in Andrew's life. Will would never have come to the village. *Would Hardeep and I have found each other without Will?*

"How is it going?" Andrew asked. "With you three."

"Everyone asks me that. No one is interested in the pub anymore or the rugby. Just us three."

Andrew blushed. There had been a time he'd made his interest in James fairly clear. Now he realised James had been juggling two men. "Sorry, none of my business."

"I'm only joking. It's going really well. We seem to just fit. If Ed is stressing, me and Arthur calm him down. If I'm getting too big for my boots, they soon sort that."

"And Arthur?"

"Oh, he has plenty of demons for us to control. Don't think he's perfect."

Andrew chewed on his lip. "So it's working then?"

"Sure is. How about you? No men on the horizon?"

Andrew sat back in his chair. He desperately wanted to talk to James about his feelings for Will and Hardeep, but they had made a pact that it would be secret, and he had no intention of breaking that. "Not just yet, but who knows what the future holds."

James patted him on the arm. "That's the spirit. The love of your life could be over the next hill."

Chapter Twenty

Hardeep wrestled with a box filled to the brim with Halloween decorations. Once September started to draw to a close, he got the old stock out and on the shelves. It seemed that people put their displays up earlier every year.

Mohinder was upstairs on the phone. He got the decorations out of the box, trying his best not to shower glittery bits all over the floor. He got shouted at every year for it, but it would take the steady hands of a brain surgeon not to spill a bit.

His mother stood at the counter looking lost.

"I will vacuum when I'm done," he said, pre-empting the onslaught.

She slowly sat on the stool by the till.

"Mum?"

She didn't answer but started to wring her hands. Throwing a plastic skeleton down, he dashed over to her. "What's the matter?"

Tears filled her eyes as she took hold of his hand. "That was your Auntie Nav on the phone."

Mohinder's older sister, Nav, had appointed herself spreader of the family news.

"Is it bad news?"

She nodded her head.

"It's Kamini."

Kamini was their baby sister. She lived on the outskirts of Mumbai in India. They had all grown up in Leeds, but Kamini had fallen in love on a visit to see family and settled out there.

"Mum?"

"She's had a heart attack," Mohinder said, bursting into tears.

Hardeep flung his arms around her and pulled her close. "How bad is it?"

"She's in hospital," his mother said, her voice muffled as she cuddled into him. "I must be with her."

Even though she had to go, things with Bina weren't great, and having to deal with her on his own made him nervous.

"Of course you do. Is Nav sorting flights?"

Mohinder wiped her eyes with a hanky. She nodded. "We're both going. I told her to book the earliest ones, no matter the cost."

"You'd better go and pack then, hadn't you?"

She pushed past him to the stairs. "Where is Satinder?"

Hardeep shook his head. "With her mother, where else? She's picking her up from school so they can have dinner together."

Mohinder narrowed her eyes. "That woman is trouble, Hardeep."

"I know she is. Believe me. But what can I do? I can't very well ban her from seeing her own daughter."

His mother seemed to have the weight of the world on her shoulders. "How about I take Sat with me? It would be good for her to meet the family and see where we come from."

Even in her lowest moments, she could still scheme, and he loved her for it. "No, thank you. She would be bored and in the way. No, this is for me to deal with."

"Hmmmm. When has that ever turned out well?"

"I'm not going to retaliate today. Off you go."

She went up the stairs and Hardeep resumed his unpacking of the stock. He and Satinder did the Halloween display together. Usually he would have to come down after she had gone to bed to rearrange things, but she enjoyed it so much, how could he complain?

He heard the back door go and went through into the small kitchen. Satinder was taking her coat off and Bina stood in the entrance hall. He hated her being in this house again. By the disdain on her face, so did she.

"Did you have a nice time?" he asked, more cheerily than he felt.

"Yes, thanks," Satinder replied, kissing him on the cheek.

The smell of stale booze washed over him and he frowned. "Have you been drinking?"

"Oh, don't be such a pain, Dad," Satinder said.

Bina allowed herself a self-satisfied smirk that made him all the angrier.

"You've been giving our underage daughter alcohol? What is the matter with you?"

"She had one glass of wine in the pub. Bloody hell, Hardeep. We didn't go on a twelve-hour bender."

That she could waltz into their lives and start acting like she was in charge made his blood boil. He turned to his daughter. "Sat, go upstairs and see your grandmother."

"Oh, what now? Has she dropped a stitch or something?"

"Less of that cheek. I won't have you showing off to your mother. Your Auntie Kamini is very ill. Granny and Auntie Nav are flying out there as soon as possible. She is very upset so try to go easy on her." His heart swelled with love as the expression on Sat's face changed to one of worry.

"Poor Granny. I'll go and help her pack."

She scampered up the stairs and into the flat. This left him alone with his ex-wife for the first time in years.

"I'd better be going," she said, moving to the door.

"Not so fast," Hardeep said.

Bina sighed. "Are you going to try and be all manly? To banish me from the kingdom of Napthwaite?"

He didn't want to be overheard and gestured for her to go into the shop. Following her, he closed the dividing door.

"I don't care where you go or what you do. But I will not let you undo all the hard work I have put in bringing up our daughter."

"I gave birth to her."

"I'm aware of that. But then you deserted her and left me to raise the wonderful young woman who is upstairs."

Bina had moved round to the customer side of the counter. She examined the stock with revulsion. "I don't remember you selling such tatt in my day," she said with a sneer.

"You barely set foot in here, so that's no surprise. I mean it, Bina. Sat is going through a difficult phase. She doesn't need you coming here, filling her head with ideas then buggering off. I will not let you hurt my daughter."

Bina's eyes flashed with anger. "She is *our* daughter. I have every right to spend time with her. Whether you like it or not, she is coming to Spain with me in the summer. She will be sixteen then so there's not a great deal you can do about it."

"I can tell you right now she will not be there for the summer. She can stay for a week and if she isn't home after that, I will come out there and drag her here myself."

"Well, well, well. The mouse has roared. You are a brave boy these days, Hardeep. Don't tell me you've got another woman in your life. Someone has released the inner caveman." She appraised him with interest. "Perhaps it's not a woman. Let's face it, you were never interested in our bed. It's a miracle I got pregnant at all."

He tried his best not to let any reaction show.

"Go on, you can tell me. I've often wondered."

"Do you find it so hard to believe that I could just have been revolted by you? The way you upset people and complain and do nothing about it? Your new man must be desperate."

She leant over the counter to slap him, but he dodged out of the way.

"Out. Now."

She stalked over to the door. "You're going to regret what you just said."

Without waiting for his reply, she left the shop, letting the door slam behind her. Hardeep exhaled. He knew she would have some form of revenge, but he had finally stood up to her. When they had been married, she had threatened to run away with the baby so many times that he had turned into a shadow to avoid upsetting her.

Once he'd closed the shop and gone upstairs, the old Satinder was very much present. She had helped her grandmother pack and set about making a meal.

Mohinder was on the phone again.

"Who is she speaking to?"

"Auntie Nav."

Mohinder finished the call.

"We've a flight in the morning. I said you'd take me to the airport."

"I'll come too," Satinder said.

Mohinder held her hand out to her granddaughter who took it. "You're a good girl. I'm going to miss you. Promise me you'll look after your father. You know what he's like."

Sat beamed. "You can count on me, Granny."

It made such a nice change to see his mother and his daughter getting on that he almost forgot about Bina and her threats. When he got into bed that night, the fear came over him again. Things had been rocky with Satinder for months now. With Bina acting like the best mother in the land, Satinder might be tempted to go away with her.

He tried to convince himself that Satinder would value his love over everything else, but a nagging doubt played over in his mind.

* * * *

The next morning, he set off on his rounds as quickly as possible. The family bond would be stretched to capacity if Mohinder missed her flight.

Will was in the garden at Thorpe Hall as Hardeep came up the path.

"Morning, handsome," Will said with a grin. "Coffee?"

"Not this morning," Hardeep said, handing him his post.

"What's up?"

He told him about his aunt and his run in with his ex-wife.

"Oh, fuck her. Satinder isn't a silly girl. Surely she must know what her mother is like."

Hardeep shook his head. "Not yet. But she will. I've no doubt about that. I'd better go. Are we meeting this week?"

Will winked. "Should be."

Hardeep desperately wanted to kiss him but even in the walled garden of the hall he didn't dare. Once he'd got home and showered, he loaded Mohinder's case into the car.

"Are you coming?" he asked Satinder. It was a Saturday and no school. He hated leaving the shop closed on a weekend, but he had no choice.

She nodded and got in the back.

"Come on, drive," Mohinder said.

"All right, Mother. We've plenty of time."

They set off to the airport. The atmosphere in the car was pretty good even with the worry of his aunt hanging over them. Once at the airport, Nav stood waiting for them. She threw her arms around every family member, sobbing. "It's just too awful," she said, clinging onto Hardeep.

"She will rally just seeing the two of you," he said.

"You're a good man, Hardeep. Thank you for bringing your mother. Now come on, we must go."

More hugs were exchanged. Standing back, Mohinder put her hands on her granddaughter's shoulders.

"Listen to me, young lady. Really listen. You need to value your father. He is the best thing in your life. No matter what."

Just as Satinder started to reply, Mohinder put her finger on her lips to silence her.

"No more talk."

With that the two older ladies set off. A wave of anxiety washed over him. Day to day life meant that they got on one another's nerves, but he loved his mother fervently. He hoped she would be okay.

To his horror, a lump appeared in his throat. He turned to Satinder, who also looked as though she might cry. "Just us then."

She nodded up at him.

* * * *

The next few days went well. Hardeep couldn't believe he had been nervous about being on his own with his daughter. They had a great time. She had even consented to playing board games with him, something they hadn't done for years.

He struggled without Mohinder though. He had to do his rounds and get back to man the shop. To her credit, Satinder had stepped up and taken on a lot of his household chores.

It had been a steady stream of customers in the shop that morning, which perked him up no end. Mohinder thought she was the only one who could turn a profit in the family? He would show her.

He was engrossed in ordering tacky Christmas decorations that would replace the Halloween ones on the shelves when his mobile vibrated.

"Hello?"

"Mr Kaur?"

"This is he."

"This is Mr Jenson from Holton High. It's about Satinder."

His heart dropped. "Is she all right?"

"I think you'd better come right away."

The honeymoon period had officially ended.

A couple of hours later and a sulky Satinder stood in the kitchen. Hardeep had closed up the shop.

"Smoking? Is this some kind of joke? You hate smoking."

"I only tried it."

He went into her bag and found a packet of cigarettes.

"Don't go in my bag," she said, wrestling it from him.

"I will not have these under my roof," he shouted, throwing them in the bin.

"Big man now Granny isn't here."

They were sliding back and he didn't know what to do to stop it. "You are grounded. I am out tonight, but I want that bedroom of yours spotless."

Satinder started to make her way upstairs. "I can't wait until I live with my mum."

He grabbed her by the wrist. "You live here."

She pulled herself free. "No, I don't. I exist here. Just so you two can have a go at me and tell me everything I do wrong. You don't care about me. You can't even cancel your stupid boys' night. Well, I'll show you. One day you'll turn around and I'll be long gone."

He let her stomp up to her room and didn't even shudder as she slammed the door so hard a dancing ghoul fell off the shelf behind the counter.

She had probably been right about him cancelling his night with Andrew and Will. But Hardeep had never needed anything more in his life. His cock twitched at the thought of the night that lay ahead.

Chapter Twenty-One

It was Wednesday night and Andrew couldn't wait to see Will and Hardeep. It had been a tough week. Not only had work been busy, but he had some planning applications and a proposal for a new playgroup to review before the next council meeting. He had really started to enjoy being a councillor.

As he plumped up the cushions on the sofa, his phone went.

"I hope that's not a cancellation," he said to Sally. "Daddy's horny." He frowned at the unknown number on the phone

"Hello?"

"Hello, stranger."

The room started to spin, and he had to grab hold of the dining chair to keep his balance.

"Andy?" said the voice on the other end.

It hit him again. It wasn't as though his life flashed before him, but memories certainly did. The jail cell. Being abused and humiliated in front of his friends.

Trying to move a drunken person who'd passed out on the street.

"Neil," Andrew said, sitting on the chair.

"Surprise. Have you missed me?"

Sally came over and nuzzled him. He stroked her. She could always sense his distress. She always had.

"What are you doing? You're not supposed to get in touch. How did you...?"

"How did I find you?"

"Yes."

Neil laughed. He had a cold, empty laugh that sent chills down Andrew's spine. It had been the punctuation to so many cruel taunts.

"You're not that good at covering your tracks," Neil sneered. "New parish councillor, is it?"

Andrew had started to shake now.

"I miss you, Andy. I search for your name sometimes and one day, boom, there's your handsome face staring up at me from your local paper. Napthwaite? Sounds like a boring dump to me."

"Well, it isn't."

"Maybe I'll come and see for myself."

"You can't. The police will –"

"The police? Come on, Andy. It's me. We don't need the bloody coppers."

"How did you get my number?"

"You want all the answers tonight, don't you? Sean, of course. I told him how desperate I was to speak to you and he took pity on me."

Sean was Neil's best friend. He hated Andrew with a passion. He also worked for a national newspaper. Andrew could just imagine him contacting the unsuspecting journalist and making up some story about wanting to interview Andrew.

"Now you have. Don't call me again."

Andrew terminated the call and switched his phone off. He stroked Sally.

"It's okay, girl. Daddy's fine."

He calmed his trembling hands down by running them through her glossy coat. The reaction to hearing Sean's voice again had shaken him to his core.

Andrew hadn't moved when the doorbell went. He jumped and opened it with the chain on. The relief at seeing Hardeep and Will almost overwhelmed him.

"What's with the chain? Expecting burglars?" Hardeep said with a smile.

"Andrew?" Will said.

The smile on both their faces dropped.

"What's wrong?" Hardeep said.

Just having them there seemed to release the shock he'd been holding back. His legs almost gave way. Hardeep grabbed him and between them they moved him to the sofa. Will crouched down between his legs as Hardeep held him by the shoulders.

"Just breathe, that's it."

Sally had come over as well, and he had three pairs of concerned eyes all poring over him. He focused on his breathing like the counsellor had told him when he'd started the long road of putting himself together after the courts had decided Neil wasn't allowed to go near him.

Neither Will nor Hardeep put him under any pressure to speak, and eventually, the panic subsided, and he wiped his eyes. "I'm sorry, guys. I wanted tonight to be nice."

Hardeep pulled him closer. "We're together. Now how about you tell us what's been going on?"

He told them everything.

"Are you going to call the police?" Hardeep asked when Andrew finished.

Andrew shook his head. "I can't face it. It was only a phone call."

"But he threatened to come here," Will said.

"I don't think he meant it. He would have been drunk."

"Do you want me to stay?" Will asked.

It would have been nice to feel another body in the bed, but he couldn't drag either of these two into it. That wasn't what Wednesday nights were about, and he didn't want to become dependent on them.

"No need," he said. "But I tell you what I do need. Desperately."

They made their way up to the bedroom. Andrew needed to disconnect from the events of the evening. He couldn't think of a better way than with these two.

But Hardeep seemed to be the horniest. He grabbed Andrew and started to unbutton his shirt. Will came up behind Hardeep and dragged his T-shirt over his head.

Hardeep ran his hand inside Andrew's shirt, letting it fall off his shoulders. His hands were all over Andrew's body before they worked their way down to his belt.

"Just get 'em off." A naked Will grinned at the other two.

Andrew gently moved Hardeep's hands away as Hardeep struggled with the belt buckle. Leaning forward to kiss him, Andrew let his trousers and boxers fall to the floor.

"Easier than messing about," he said. He kicked his clothes into the corner and joined Will on the bed. "Hurry up, slow coach."

Hardeep took the rest of his clothes off. He lay down on the other side of Will. Andrew loved the contrast between the two. Will didn't have much hair whereas Hardeep had a gorgeous hairy chest.

They became a mass of limbs entwined and mouths seeking others as they rolled around on the bed.

Andrew took hold of Hardeep's hard cock and started to suck. Hardeep lay on his back and Will moved over so he straddled his body. Andrew carried on sucking Hardeep but couldn't take his eyes from Will's hole that was inches from his face.

He let the cock drop and turned his attention to Will. He licked his ass cheeks before delving between them. This time he heard Will make a noise as he worked him as hard as he could.

Will's hairless arse was perfection and Andrew couldn't get enough. He reached up for Will's hips, going deeper with his tongue. Letting his hand drop, he palmed Hardeep's balls, kneading them in time with his tongue. The feeling of being in control of these two amazing men made his cock swell even more. He wanted desperately to fuck Will, but he had other ideas first. He grabbed a condom and lube from the nightstand. "Don't fucking move," he whispered.

Not that he had to. Hardeep and Will were lost in their kiss, Will holding Hardeep's arms above his head.

Andrew rolled the condom onto Hardeep's cock and gently applied the lube to Will's hole. Both men squirmed in pleasure. He guided Hardeep's dick so the tip teased Will. He slipped a finger inside, finding Will's prostate and rubbing.

Will released Hardeep from the kiss and leant back. Andrew held Hardeep firm as Will moved down his dick. It was so arousing seeing it disappear into Will's ass.

Will reached the base and let out a moan. "Oh, God. That's good."

Will started to ride Hardeep. There must have been something in the air because there was no slow build up. Will wanted this. He rode fast.

Hardeep's face screamed pure bliss as Will made the bed shake. Tugging at his own cock, Andrew contented himself with watching the scene unfold but when Will turned and held his hand out, he couldn't resist.

Will massaged Andrew's cock, who reached forward and returned the favour, at the same time Andrew thrust his lips onto Will's and kissed him furiously.

"Will," Hardeep cried out before arching his back.

But he didn't stop. He expertly took the man to orgasm. Seconds later, Will's body tensed and he came furiously in his hands.

Andrew moved away from the other two and went to get a towel he had left on the chest of drawers. He threw it to them and disappeared into the bathroom.

Examining the flushed face in the mirror, he wondered why he hadn't wanted to come. He always prided himself on finishing but today it seemed unnecessary.

As he walked back into the bedroom, the other two stopped talking. He bet they had been asking themselves the same question.

"What?" he asked.

Will held his arm out and Andrew cuddled into his side.

"You didn't come."

Andrew kissed him on the shoulder. "No but you two certainly did."

They settled into a comfortable position. Andrew flung his leg over Will, then reached for Hardeep's hand and took it. He wanted them to know there was nothing wrong.

"I can't be too late," Hardeep said. "I'm on my own with Satinder. Well, that's if she hasn't run away to be with her mother by now."

"Things still bad?" Will asked.

"Like you wouldn't believe. We had a huge row before I came out. She thinks she just exists with me, but she could live with her mother."

"Pretty harsh," Andrew said.

"What are you going to do?" Will asked.

Hardeep exhaled. "Fuck knows."

"Have you tried talking to her?" Will replied.

"I've tried many times, but it just ends in arguments. Every single time."

Andrew thought about being a teenager. His father had been a market trader and in an uber masculine world, a gay son had not been on the agenda. They had argued to the point where one day, Andrew just left. He hadn't seen his father since.

"It's normal that she's in awe of her mother," he said. "She's built her up to be this perfect person for most of her life. It won't take long for Bina to show her that she isn't."

Hardeep moved onto his side. "That's just the thing, though. I can't bear to think of her being hurt."

"I'm not sure you can control that," Will said. "Instead of being the person who comes down hard on her and tries to get her to see reality, how about being the man who she loves the most in the world? I'm not saying you have to compete with Bina. Give her enough rope. Satinder needs to remember why she loves you."

Hardeep nuzzled into Will's neck and they closed their eyes.

Andrew watched them doze off.

He had a terrible fear that Satinder wasn't the only one who loved Hardeep. Like it or not, these two men were finding their way into the heart he had vowed to keep locked tight. He couldn't tell if it was hearing Neil's voice again that had made him feel vulnerable or if he were on this road already.

He snuggled in next to them. His life was out of his control again. He couldn't decide whether to let it happen or run.

Chapter Twenty-Two

Hardeep crept into the lounge. He frowned as he saw Satinder lying asleep on the couch with an empty bottle of wine on the table. She had never touched alcohol before and certainly not on a school night. At first he wanted to shake her and demand to know what the hell had got into her. But then he heard Will's voice from earlier. Getting angry with her would only result in a huge row, especially if she had had a drink.

Swallowing down his anger, he walked over to the sofa. He lifted her legs and slid underneath them, resting her feet on his lap. Satinder stirred and opened her eyes. She jumped when she saw her father staring back at her.

"Dad."

"Who else?"

"I fell asleep."

"Did that have anything to do with it?" he said, nodding his head towards the wine bottle.

She had the decency to look ashamed. "I was going to get rid of it."

"I'm sure you were."

He started to rub her feet like he had when she was a little girl.

"If you're going to have a go at me…"

"Am I that bad?"

Beeb stood on the floor next to them, trying to get up to no avail. Satinder reached down and pulled him onto her chest, cuddling him.

"I know you don't want me to see Mum."

Hardeep sighed. "It's not that I don't want you to see her, Sat."

"What is it then?"

She was still so young. He wished he could keep her as a child forever, but she would be demanding more and more freedom as time went on. He could either go along with it or lose her.

"Your mum hurt me badly when she left. I had such a lot of debt and you were only young. If it hadn't been for Granny, I don't know what I would have done. Now she just arrives and is demanding a place in your life. Can't you see it from my point of view?"

Satinder seemed to be struggling with so much. "Are you saying I should tell her to leave?"

As if he could ever ask her to do that, even if a tiny part of him screamed *Yes*.

"Not at all. I'm just very scared for you. I'm your dad and I love you more than anything on this whole planet. I've protected you from everything since the day you were born. It's hard for me to stand by and watch you possibly get hurt."

"She might not hurt me. You don't know that."

"That's very true. I know you need a mother and you've missed her. I'll do you a deal. I won't make trouble about you seeing her, but I will be watching.

Very closely. If there's anything at all that doesn't seem right to you, I want you to promise you'll come and talk to me."

"Mum says you're jealous."

"That sounds like your mother. For the record I'm not. I know how much we love each other. Nothing and no one can get in the way of that."

Satinder thought for a second. "It's nice to hear you say that. I thought you just wanted to shout at me and go out with your friends."

"That's silly talk. I was thinking... How about we get this place smartened up for Granny coming home? You and me?"

Satinder sat up. "Can I choose the colours?"

"Within reason."

"It's been nice just you and me though, hasn't it?"

Ever since the teenage years hit, Satinder and his mother had been friends one minute and enemies the next.

"Your granny loves you too, you know."

Satinder sighed. "I know, it's just..."

"What?"

"I disappoint her."

"Darling, you do nothing of the sort. She's just a very forthright woman."

And the understatement of the year goes to Hardeep Kaur.

"Dad..."

"Yes, love?"

"It doesn't matter."

"No, go on. You can tell me anything you know."

She stared at him as though something big wanted to escape her mouth. He braced himself for a bombshell, but the moment had passed and her face relaxed.

"It's nothing. I love you."

"I love you too. Now time for bed. I may have let you get away with drinking on a school night—which is a one-off by the way—but I'm not letting you stay up much later. You're not an adult yet."

She laughed and shifted Beeb, and he curled up on a cushion. She got off the sofa and kissed the top of his head. "Thanks, Dad."

With that she went into her bedroom. It made a nice change that the door gently closed instead of being slammed. Perhaps Will had been right. Talking rather than shouting made a huge difference.

* * * *

The next day, Dean Poole from across the street had come to help out in the post office while Hardeep did his rounds. He had resigned himself to opening the shop late with Mohinder being away, but Dean had come across and offered.

"It's ever so good of you to help out like this, Dean. Are you sure your mum can spare you?"

Dean had an ironed shirt on and Hardeep detected gel in his hair.

"It's okay, Mr Kaur. She's doing a stocktake and says I just get under her feet."

"Well, I'm very grateful indeed. If anyone comes in for the post office, just tell them I'll be back soon. I'm sure you can handle the shop."

Dean looked around, taking in the place.

"Is Satinder in?" he asked hopefully.

It all became clear. Hardeep tried unsuccessfully to hide a smile. "Not at the moment. She's gone to school."

Dean's face dropped a little.

"But she's promised to clean the window display when she gets home. Imagine how chuffed she would be if it had already been done."

The young lad perked up. "Consider it done, Mr Kaur."

"It's Hardeep. The cleaning things are in the kitchen."

Hardeep left Dean filling a bucket. Satinder had never cleaned the window display in her life. They were usually the domain of Mohinder. Hardeep chuckled to himself as he set off around the village.

The clock struck nine and he realised he would have to get a move on. He did his round at breakneck speed. Mrs Turnbull had tried to entice him in with promise of a freshly baked cherry cake. Usually he did go in, to get all the news of the village, but today he had to get back and she settled for putting a foil-wrapped slab into his bag.

Even at Andrew's he felt relieved to see he and Sally were out.

He arrived at the post office, out of breath and sweaty.

"Everything been all right, Dean?"

Dean perched on Mohinder's stool behind the till, reading a comic.

"Yes…Hardeep. I even sold Becky from The King's some stamps."

"Very good. The windows are wonderful. Thank you for doing them."

The door chime went and Hardeep's face darkened.

Oblivious, Dean puffed his chest up proudly. "Will you tell Satinder I did the windows?"

"Yes, of course," Hardeep said, distracted by the figure that stared at him.

"Hello, Hardeep. I'm not late, am I?"

"No, Bina. You're right on time. Dean, could I impose on your good nature a little while longer? I need to speak to this lady upstairs."

Dean looked from one to the other. He clearly recognised her but simply nodded and resumed reading his comic.

Hardeep lifted the counter and gestured Bina to go through. "Go on upstairs. I'm sure you can remember the way." As much as he didn't want her infecting their family home, he needed to do this. He followed her into the lounge. She stalked over to the window and turned to face him.

"You haven't changed very much. It feels just like home."

Hardeep stood by the door. "It's our home, not yours."

Beeb scratched at his bedroom door. Hardeep went over and let him free. Ever the inquisitive little pup, he ran over to Bina.

"What a cute little dog," she said, bending down to stroke him.

To Hardeep's joy, Beeb backed off, growling. He made a mental note to give Beeb a double portion for his dinner that night.

Bina didn't seem phased. She straightened up and held her hands out. "You summoned me, so I have come. What is it you want, Hardeep?"

"I thought we should speak alone seeing as we share a child. A child you've taken it upon yourself to disrupt at a time when she is getting ready to take important exams next summer."

She sighed and glanced out of the window, seemingly bored.

"It is a difficult time in her life, Bina. You'd know if you had paid attention for the last few years."

"I see. The big Hardeep declares that I'm a bad influence and should disappear to Spain again. Is that it?"

She had such a talent for twisting his words. They had shared many a shouting match in this very room. "Don't be so melodramatic," he said. "I'm simply saying she isn't some prize to be fought over because you remembered you had a daughter. I absolutely will not let you disrupt her life."

A nasty gleam crept across her face. "This caveman act is all very endearing, but it bored me last time and it bores me today."

Hardeep would not let her wind him up. He had vowed to keep this strictly business and that's what he would do. "Save your petty insults. I couldn't care less what you think of me. What I do care about is how you treat our daughter. I'm prepared to trust that even you have a modicum of maternal instinct."

"That's very generous of you."

"I will give you one chance, Bina. If you hurt my daughter, I will make sure you never get within a county of her."

Bina strode over to him and ran her hand down his chest. "I could almost find you attractive."

He pushed her hand away. "One chance."

"That's all I need. I've come to make things better not worse. Don't you believe me?" She didn't wait for a reply as she walked to the doorway, then turned and glared at him. "I'll see you real soon."

He had no doubt they would be seeing her soon. He just hoped he had done the right thing letting her in.

Chapter Twenty-Three

Will sat at the island in the kitchen. The coffee had brewed and he had stolen a moment with the newspaper. Sadly, that newspaper was *The Telegraph*, his father's daily fix for almost fifty years. He sighed as he flicked through the pages.

The door opened and Matthew came shuffling through. Will leapt up to help him. "Dad, you should have shouted."

"I can go where I like in my own house, thank you," he replied.

Will steered him to a stool and purposefully didn't react when Matthew shrugged him away. He'd only done that once he had reached safety, but Will knew better than to mention it. He dashed over to the coffee machine and poured him a cup, placing it down in front of him.

"Anything decent in there?" Matthew said, nodding to the newspaper.

"In here? You're kidding, aren't you? I don't know why you insist on getting this right-wing rag."

Matthew raised his eyebrows. "I can just imagine the talk around this village if I changed my order at Brockbank's to *Socialist Weekly*."

Will winked. "It would cause a commotion though."

Matthew huffed and took a sip of his drink.

Will resumed flicking through the paper. He had been meaning to have a conversation with his father and this seemed like the perfect opportunity.

"Dad?" he ventured.

"What?"

"I've been thinking."

"Oh, you have, have you?"

"I wondered if it would be a good idea to put this place on the market."

His father's hand slamming down on the island made him jump and he spilt coffee down himself. "Dad? What are you doing?"

"What the hell are *you* doing, my lad?" His father looked furious.

"It was just a thought. You have the cottages in the village. One of those would be far more suitable for you now —"

"This is the second time you've tried this and I won't have it. This house has been in our family for generations. You want me to the be the one to lose it?"

"So you'd prefer that fell to me then?" Will spat back.

For a second Matthew stopped in his tracks. Clearly he hadn't thought past his own imagined responsibilities for this pile of bricks. "What?" he managed.

"I won't continue with this house, Dad. It's best to be honest. If you think you're saving it by keeping hold of it, you're not."

Matthew turned a horrid shade of red and Will panicked that he had gone too far. He wasn't a well man after all. Why did his father always bring this spiteful side out in him? Climbing off the stool, Matthew walked silently out of the room.

"That went marvellously," Will said to Titus. He thought it best to give his father time to calm down so set to work making his favourite dish. His mouth always got him into trouble, but his cooking usually saved the day.

A couple of hours later and he dished a bubbling portion of gooey lasagne onto a plate. He had heard nothing from Matthew so hoped this would go some way to mending bridges.

He poked his head around the study door. Matthew lay fast asleep on the couch, a book open on his chest. Will put the plate down on the desk and stood, watching his father's chest rise and fall.

What will life be like without him?

Their relationship had weathered more storms than Napthwaite church steeple, but Matthew was also the only constant in Will's life. How would it feel to be totally cast adrift? "I'm sorry, Dad," he whispered.

Even though they lived in a huge house, he felt claustrophobic. Putting on his coat, he let himself out then walked down the drive. The leaves were on the turn now and blowing everywhere. Even though it meant that a harsh winter would soon be here, the beauty couldn't be ignored.

Will lost himself in his thoughts as he walked and soon found himself on Queen Street, by the post office. He hadn't really intended to come here but now he had, he went to the door and knocked.

A young girl covered in paint splatters answered. "Hello?"

"Hello, Satinder. Is your dad at home?"

She gave him a suspicious look before shouting for her father. "Are you one of his new Wednesday friends then?" she asked, leaning against the doorframe.

"I suppose I am," Will said. He had never really got on with teenagers.

"He doesn't say much about you."

"He talks about you all the time," Will said with what he hoped was an endearing smile.

A nervous Hardeep appeared behind his daughter. "Will? Are you okay?"

Will realised this had been a mistake. Hardeep had been very clear about wanting to keep his worlds separate and he should have respected that. As hard as it would be in a tiny village. "I'm sorry, I was out for a walk and thought I'd call in. But you're busy, forgive me."

Without waiting for an answer, he set off down the side alley and onto Queen Street. It didn't really surprise him when he heard footsteps and a panting Hardeep caught him up.

"Hang on there, Usain Bolt," Hardeep panted. "What's up?"

"Oh nothing. I had a row with Dad…again. But it's not your problem. You've got enough to deal with."

They walked onto the green.

"Don't be daft. We've only got the glossing left to do and I hate that bit. I've promised Satinder fifty quid if she's finished by the time I get back. Let's give her a fighting chance and go and see Andrew."

"That's not a bad idea. I've come to a bit of a decision, and it affects both of you."

Hardeep frowned at Will. "What do you mean?"

"It's easier to tell you both at once. Now tell me what rooms you're decorating."

Hardeep rattled on about the colours they had chosen for the flat as they walked up the lane to Andrew's house. Will hoped Andrew wouldn't mind them just calling in. They opened the squeaky gate which immediately set Sally off barking.

"I wish he'd get that bloody gate seen to," Hardeep grumbled. "Every time I come to deliver, it sets her off."

"Maybe Sally likes an early warning system. She's not getting any younger."

They knocked on the door. A face appeared at the window, then disappeared. They heard about three locks being opened on the door. Will hadn't realised Andrew was this security conscious. *Is this a new thing?*

"Is it Wednesday and no one told me?" he said, confused.

"No, this man of mystery needs to tell us something," Hardeep said to him.

"You'd better come in then."

They both went into the house. Apparently, Andrew made a special effort for Wednesday nights. Plates were piled high on the side in the kitchen and newspapers spread across the sofa.

"Sorry for the mess," Andrew said.

"You should be," Hardeep replied, looking around.

"Unannounced callers have to take me as they find me." Andrew scowled.

Will remembered the locks on the doors. "Have you heard from Neil again?"

"Course not. He wouldn't dare," Andrew said, sitting. "Doesn't hurt to be safe though, does it?"

Hardeep sat next to him, but a nervous Will stood by the fireplace.

"I can stay with you if you're not feeling safe," Will continued.

"I said I'm fine, didn't I? So come on, out with it. What's the big announcement?"

Will sighed. "There's no easy way to say this, but I'm going to New York immediately. Ange is going over there next week, and I've agreed to join her."

"Have you got a job?" Hardeep said.

"No. I can finish up at The King's so anyone can come and take over. Dad is on the road to recovery now and, to be honest, I think my being here has started to hinder that. He needs routine. We wind each other up too much. I thought I was going to give him another bloody heart attack today."

A pale Andrew didn't speak and Hardeep seemed lost in thought.

"Perhaps you're right," Hardeep said.

"What do you mean?" Will asked.

"This is a sign. You need to go and find your dreams in New York, and I need to spend more time with my daughter. Bina is circling, and I should be watching her like a hawk. Instead, I'm always thinking about coming up here. Let's face it, if my darling ex-wife got even a hint of what we get up to, she would stick the knife in."

They both turned to Andrew who had been silent.

"Andrew?" Will said.

Andrew got up. "You're right. It couldn't last forever but it's been fun, yeah? I'm sorry, guys, but I have a parish council meeting tonight so..."

Will hadn't even thought that Andrew would be busy. "Oh yeah, right."

Andrew practically pushed them out of the house and locked the door behind them.

"I don't think he took that very well," Hardeep said as they made their way down the path.

"He's always banging on about it being all fun and no emotions."

They set off down the lane.

"It's sad though," Will continued. "I really like you two. In another world, eh?"

Hardeep slung his arm around Will's shoulder. "In another world."

Chapter Twenty-Four

Hardeep had seemed upset as they walked down the lane from Andrew's so Will persuaded him to come to The King's for a drink. The pub was pretty busy but they found themselves a little nook in the corner. Hardeep nursed a pint.

"So, Bina?"

Hardeep sighed. "She's getting under Sat's skin and I don't trust her. But I took your advice and am going for the softer approach. If I forbid them from seeing each other, I'm just turning her into a martyr."

Will took a swig of his drink. "I think you're doing the right thing. Chances are Satinder is going to be let down, but she will need you more than ever then. If you've closed yourself off, that will hurt her more."

Hardeep nodded. "I feel bad leaving Andrew like that. It will be weird us still being in the same village."

Will hadn't really thought what it would be like for the two of them once he had gone. He felt guilty that he had a new start to aim for. "You never know, further down the line."

Hardeep shook his head. "I think Andrew has made it very clear he isn't the relationship type. Besides it wouldn't be the same without you there. No, I think it's best we all break now."

"Hardeep, will you do me a favour?"

"Of course. What do you need?"

Will's heart melted. Even as he dealt with the breaking up of his first gay experience and worried about his daughter, Hardeep didn't even wait to find out what he wanted. He was such a kind man.

"Could you keep an eye on my dad? If he starts failing or if he needs anything at all, you'll get in touch?"

Hardeep put his hand on Will's leg under the table. "Goes without saying."

"You're a wonderful person, Hardeep. Once this is all sorted and Satinder is off being a uni student, I really hope you find the man of your dreams."

Hardeep looked down. "I doubt that will happen but thank you. I'm sure you'll find a decent chap in New York. A handsome man like you."

"That just leaves Andrew. What did you make of all the locks tonight? He's never had those on before."

A man came into the pub, banging the door. Everyone stopped their conversation. Will didn't recognise his face as he approached the bar. He couldn't quite hear what he spoke to Becky about, but she seemed to be giving him directions. The guy stomped out of the pub. Will didn't like the expression on his face.

"Another?"

Hardeep nodded.

Will approached the bar. "Same again, please, Beck," he said. "Who was that man?"

Becky started to pull the pints. "Some visitor. He thought they held the parish council here because James is chair."

Will frowned. "What does he want with the parish council?"

"He's a reporter from Holton. Wants to do a feature on villages at Christmas or something. I sent him down to the village hall. Is something wrong?"

He handed over a note. "Keep the change. No nothing wrong. He just seemed a bit off."

Becky took the money. "If I worried about every off bloke who came in here, I'd have lost my hair years ago."

Will returned to Hardeep with the drinks.

"What's the matter?"

"Oh nothing. I've been living in cities too long. I'm getting paranoid."

The second drink led to a third and a fourth. The clock struck ten and a slightly unsteady Hardeep and Will left the pub.

Standing on the green, Will didn't want to leave Hardeep. "Will you be okay? I'm not going until the weekend. If you need anything, give me a shout."

Hardeep smiled. "I know what I need, but we're not doing that anymore."

Will winked. "We could always arrange a meet up for one last time."

"Sounds good to me."

"I'll ring Andrew. We have one more Wednesday after all."

Hardeep embraced him. "You'll never know what you've done for me, Will Johnstone."

Will kissed his neck. "All in a day's work. Now get off to your daughter, and I'll see you before I go."

They parted and Will set off home. The stars shone brightly in the clear sky. One of the best things about being up here was no light pollution. He got his phone out and dialled Andrew's number.

It went straight to voicemail.

Will frowned. It wasn't that late, and Andrew always stayed up watching some crap on the TV. He tried again.

"Hello?"

"Andrew?"

"Yes?"

He sounded odd.

"Is everything all right?"

"It's fine. I'm just tired. Did you want something?"

It wasn't like him to be this gruff. "I thought I'd check on you. Hardeep and I had a drink in The King's, and we were thinking of one more Wednesday night. What do you think?"

There was no response.

"Andrew?"

"I'm tired, Will. I've had a long night. We'll see, yeah?"

"Oh yeah, fine. You sure you're all right? I can still come and stay if you want."

"No. I told you, I'm tired. I'm going to bed in a minute."

"Fair enough. Sorry to have disturbed you —"

Before he could say anything else, the line went dead. Will didn't like this. He had reached the gates of Thorpe Hall and for a second, he thought about turning round and going to Andrew's.

"Don't be so stupid, Johnstone," he muttered to himself. Andrew had sounded pissed off, so a slightly drunk man knocking on his door probably wouldn't make that much better. As he put his key in the door, a niggling doubt festered in his mind. Something wasn't right. He would get himself a glass of wine and text Hardeep, see what he thought.

But when he wandered into the kitchen, his heart almost stopped. Matthew lay prone across the floor. Titus lay next to him and growled at first until he saw it was Will, then he got up and whined.

Will dropped to his knees. "Dad? Dad can you hear me?"

Frantically grabbing his wrist, he felt for a pulse. It was there. Will's heart rate started to return to normal. He checked his father, seeing a cut on his head. He rifled through his pocket and found his phone. With a shaking hand, he dialled nine-nine-nine.

The next hour passed in a blur. Will sat with his father on the cold kitchen floor as they waited for an ambulance to arrive. It took ages. Another side effect of living in the countryside. He had cried for joy when the blue lights illuminated the kitchen.

Now he found himself in a dimly lit cubicle in a busy A&E department. His father slept with a huge bandage on his head. Will had sobered up pretty quickly and sat at the end of the bed, watching his father's chest rise and fall.

So many emotions ran through him. Anger with himself for being so selfish. Sadness that his father's capacities were so reduced. Indecision between what he'd wanted and what he should do.

It got to nearly midnight. The nurse who attended Matthew suggested that Will went home — they would be transferring his father to a ward as soon as they found a bed and he would probably sleep. Matthew refused. He didn't want him waking up and not seeing a familiar face.

As it turned out, he didn't have long to wait. About half an hour later, Matthew started to stir. Will dashed up the bed and took his father's hand.

"What's going on?" he managed.

Will's heart ached as he saw the fear on his face. "It's fine. You had a bit of a fall."

With his other hand, Matthew reached up to feel the bandage around his forehead and winced.

"You banged your head. The doctors are keeping you in tonight, just to make sure everything is good." Will smiled as his father locked eyes with him.

"What are you doing here?"

Oh God, he's got amnesia. "I've been here for weeks, Dad."

"I know that, you idiot. I mean, why are you here? I thought you'd be getting ready for New York."

Will sat at the side of the bed. He squeezed the hand in his. "I'm not sure that's a good idea now."

Matthew sighed. "I'm not having you change your plans out of pity for me."

The old stubbornness hadn't gone anywhere. Will didn't know if that were a good or bad thing. He had no intention of getting into an argument, so he let the comment go and sat there in silence.

"She wouldn't recognise me nowadays," Matthew said.

Will frowned. "Who?"

"Your mother. Did she tell you where we met?"

"No."

Matthew's eyes softened as he became lost in his memories. "We met in the departure lounge at Schiphol Airport. She was flying to New York and I to Bangkok.

We both went to sit on the same seat. Of course, I let her have it, but she offered to share it. When you're half perched on a chair, you can't help but strike up a conversation."

He couldn't imagine them both sitting precariously on a chair, but that was typical of his mother. She would have shared anything with anyone.

"Then what did you do?" Will asked.

"I got her address of course. When a beautiful woman is thrown across your path like that, you grab her with both hands."

A tear escaped from his eye. Will grabbed a tissue and tenderly wiped it away.

"I loved her with all my soul, Will. But I've let her down and I'll never forgive myself for it."

"What do you mean?"

"I never loved you like I should have."

Will's heart started to thud heavily in his chest. His father never spoke like this. "I know you love me."

Matthew tried to sit up, but Will gently kept him in place.

"I should tell you. Every single day. But when you were younger, to look at you broke my heart. The only way I could deal with it was to retreat into myself. I'm so desperately sorry."

A nurse popped her head around the curtain. "Ah we're awake. That's a good sign. We've found you a bed, so we'll be moving you up there in the next ten minutes or so. I'm afraid you'll have to go then," she said, turning to Will.

He nodded and she left them in peace. "That's me thrown out then," he said.

But his father gripped tightly onto his hand. "Don't go."

"Dad, I have to. They won't let me on the ward where other patients are sleeping."

"No, I mean, don't go to New York."

He couldn't believe that his father was opening up his vulnerability like this. In that moment, Will loved him more than he ever had. "Dad…"

"You're right. Let's put the house on the market. It's time new blood ran through those corridors. Will, let's make up for lost time."

The tears were flowing out of both of them now.

"Do you mean this? I thought I got under your feet."

"Oh, you do that all right. That's why we'll have a house each. They're only across the road from each other, so you can keep an eye on me but keep your independence. It will save you trudging up to Andrew's cottage every Wednesday."

To his shock, he detected a glint in his father's eye.

"Think about it," he finished.

Will didn't need to. "It's a deal."

"Are you sure now? New York is exciting."

Will kissed the back of his father's hand. "Finding you again is more exciting."

Chapter Twenty-Five

The television blared out some late-night rubbish as Andrew nursed a whisky. Will had sounded so full of hope for his new life in America. The sadness that had engulfed Andrew earlier didn't show any sign of disappearing. He had sat through the parish council meeting on autopilot.

He only had himself to blame. He had gone on and on about their arrangement not being anything but fun, but now he felt lost at the thought of losing them. Will would be gone soon but facing Hardeep in the village every day would be torture. Andrew didn't begrudge Hardeep from focusing on his daughter, but it left him alone.

He glanced over at Sally, who lay sleeping in her bed as though she didn't have a care in the world. Perhaps they should move somewhere new. He would miss Lisa, but she could visit. Sally growled in her sleep. She had stuck with him through thick and thin. He remembered the day Neil had brought her home, a little ball of fur. She had been another grand gesture of apology after he'd lost his temper. A way to try and persuade Andrew to ignore the black eye in the mirror every morning.

Neil suddenly filled his thoughts. He hadn't told the others, but he'd had countless phone calls which had gone through to voicemail. Neil being back in his life, however small, freaked him out. Walking up the road from the meeting that evening, he had been spooked that someone was following him. Twice he'd whirled round to look behind him. Once he could have sworn he'd seen someone dart behind a bush but, after standing still for a few minutes, he couldn't see anything. Taking a swig of his whisky, he tried to dismiss the thoughts. Paranoia had clearly set in now. He'd finish this and curl up with Sally in bed. He needed to put this day to rest.

He drained the glass and got up to put it in the kitchen. He stopped and frowned as he heard sirens blaring through the quiet night. Living in a village, everyone stopped still when they heard that noise. Chances were they would know whoever needed help. Andrew hoped it wasn't anyone he truly cared about.

Placing the glass on the draining board, he realised that there were people in that village that he cared about, and the number was growing. He hadn't done anything to persuade Will to stay or Hardeep to try and reconcile his true self with his life.

Sally loped up to him and glanced expectantly at her food bowl.

"Nice try," he said, scratching behind her ears. "I don't know, girl. Should I have put up a fight?"

No doubt this would be a worry that would prevent him from sleeping that night. He flicked the light off and walked across the lounge to the stairs. He almost leapt out of his skin as there was a loud knock at the door.

The clock had just struck eleven.

"Who the hell is that?"

Sally growled. He didn't want her to go dashing out into the night and the next hour be spent coaxing her inside. He gently pulled her over to the stairs and closed the door.

Another knock made him jump.

"Who is it?"

Not a sound could be heard. Adrenalin pumped through him. What if he hadn't been mistaken earlier? A large stick which an over-ambitious Sally had brought back from their afternoon walk lay by the door. He picked it up and gingerly opened the door. Everything was pitch-dark outside. Reaching across the wall, he turned the outside lights on, illuminating the lawn that ran in front of the house.

He couldn't see anything. Just as he was about to give up, he heard a rock land on his car.

"Who's there?" he shouted.

More silence. The hairs on his neck stood up.

Another rock bounced off his car.

This time anger took the place of anxiety and he darted out to the driveway. It would be kids. He wished he'd put the car in the garage.

"Whoever it is, I'll kick your bloody arse."

His eyes getting used to the dark, he saw the two stones by his front tyre. He couldn't see anything.

What am I doing?

As sense flooded back to him, he went towards the house. The police had said to contact them if anything out of the ordinary happened. This was definitely that so he would ring the number for Holton Police. Plus he would make sure Sally didn't leave his side tonight.

Going into the lounge, he froze. There on his sofa sat Neil. Sally clawed at the door, barking.

"Better let her in," Neil sneered. "I'm sure she's missed her other daddy."

Andrew couldn't move. Neil shifted to get more comfortable as though he'd lived there all his life.

"Close the door. You're letting all the cold air in," he said.

It was then that Andrew saw the big knife laid across his lap. "Neil, you shouldn't be here," he said.

Neil got up from the sofa and walked up to Andrew. He knew he should run but he couldn't move. As he got closer to him, Andrew could smell the cloying scent of the aftershave Neil always wore. The musky smell reminded him so vividly of all the arguments they'd had over the years. His heart raced as Neil closed the door.

"I wanted to see you. There's not a law against it," he said, leaning in closely so Andrew could feel his breath on his neck. "I've missed you, baby."

"There is a law against it. The police said —"

Neil shoved him against the door. "The police can go fuck themselves. What they don't know won't hurt them."

Andrew looked into his cold eyes. How had he ever thought he'd found love in them?

"I won't tell you again. Sit down."

He had no choice but to comply. The room that he had created as his sanctuary now became a prison as he allowed himself to be frogmarched over to the sofa. Neil pushed him so he tripped and fell onto it.

"Steady on, Andrew. I only came to talk, but if you want to get more physical, I'm up for it." Neil laughed.

Andrew scrambled up. Neil sat at the other end, absentmindedly stroking the hilt of the knife.

"So how have you been?" Neil asked. Andrew couldn't believe he could talk to him as though it were a casual visit.

"Fine. Neil, please. You'll get into trouble."

"If you'd answered my calls, I wouldn't have had to come, would I? But you think you're too good for me now, don't you?"

Sally whined at the door.

"Aren't you going to let her in?"

Andrew shook his head. "She'll go for you and you'll hurt her."

"She always did like you more. Oh well, you can't win them all, I guess. Why did you do it? We were all right, but you had to go crying to the police like a little bitch."

Even though he was terrified, Andrew couldn't believe this. "You had me arrested, Neil. Did you expect me to lie to protect you?"

Quick as a flash Neil leapt forward, his body pressing on Andrew's. The knife pressed against his torso.

"That's exactly what I expected, you little fuck. We always made things better after one of our falling-outs. Then you've disappeared and some copper tells me I'm not allowed to look for you. I've got a record, thanks. You know they do police checks at work. Newsflash. I lost my job."

Andrew had heard that Neil had been fired from his job at the care home. He had presumed it had been down to his temper — he hadn't realised it had been a link in the chain of their hideous relationship. "Neil, I'm sorry. I didn't think…"

Neil kissed him, the cloud of anger disappearing instantly. "It feels good to have you underneath me again."

To his horror, Andrew felt Neil harden as his groin pressed against his thigh.

"Honestly, you need to go. I've got a friend coming."

"It's nearly midnight. Don't give me that shit." Neil moved so his body was closer to Andrew's, and he ran his free hand across Andrew's chest. "I've missed you."

The revulsion almost overpowered Andrew. Regardless of the danger, he batted Neil's hand away. "Get off me. I'll give you one more chance to go."

Tears appeared in Neil's eyes. He had always been prone to mood swings, but nothing like this. It made the fear all the greater for Andrew.

"Why are you being like this? I've spent over a year looking for you. I even thought you might have gone abroad. Then here you are, in the middle of fuck knows where. Parish councillor, eh? Couldn't resist the newspaper though, could you?"

Damn that bloody interview. "I've made a new life for myself."

"Make room for me. Please, Andrew. We get each other. You know we do."

The wind whipped up outside and branches tapped on the window. If he bolted for it, Neil would expect him to go for the front door. Instead he'd go for the kitchen and out of the garage that he'd left open.

"Okay, you're right. Let's talk," Andrew said as calmly as he could manage. "How about I fix us a drink?"

Neil moved away from him. Andrew breathed a sigh of relief when he could no longer feel the body heat from him.

"That's more like it."

Andrew got up. "What do you want?"

"Coffee. Strong. Something tells me I'll be up all night. Doing what is up to you." Neil winked.

Andrew managed a weak smile. He could only focus on getting out of that building. Fighting every urge to run, he walked calmly to the kitchen. With a shaking hand, he filled the kettle and set it on to boil.

Glancing through to the lounge showed him Neil was still sitting. Andrew crept over to the door that connected to the garage and tried it. It was locked. Then he realised he had left through there that morning as he'd taken the recycling on his way to work. The key was in the other side.

"Is the milk in the garage then?" Neil said behind him.

Andrew had trapped himself in his own house. Fear and rage boiled inside him. He would not accept this. He grabbed the almost boiling kettle and threw the contents at Neil. Neil let out a scream as some of the red-hot water hit him.

Seeing his opportunity, Andrew barged past him towards the door. But Neil was too quick for him, and Andrew screamed out in pain as the knife slashed at his back, cutting through his shirt. He fell against the door, banging his head. Then everything went black.

Chapter Twenty-Six

The shop had been pretty quiet. Hardeep fiddled with his phone, checking the group chat. They hadn't heard from Andrew since the night before and Hardeep had started to worry. Mrs Turnbull had come in first thing to give him the news that Matthew Johnstone had had a fall. He had messaged Will and got a short reply that his father was fine. He didn't like to bother him with worry about Andrew, but surely Will would notice the radio silence?

The back door went. Bina had come to take Satinder out to lunch. The forced friendliness had been quite the struggle as he'd waved them off. He had to admit that hearing her voice and her not being in floods of tears made him relax a little more.

"Mum, will you just leave it, please?"

She might not be in tears, but she didn't sound happy. He went to the doorway, but something stopped him. *What is Bina up to?*

"I'm only saying he's a handsome lad. Why don't you go out with him?"

"Because I don't want to. Liz Poole is awful, and I don't want anything to do with them."

"Liz was always all right when I lived here. What's your problem with her?"

"She was awful with Dean's uncle and his two partners."

"His two partners?" Bina said, mockingly. "His two perverts, more like."

"Leave me alone."

Hardeep shuddered as he heard his daughter's footsteps banging up the stairs. He walked through the doorway just in time to bar Bina's way. "Where do you think you're going?"

"Snooping on other people's conversations, are we?" she said.

Hardeep stood on the bottom step. "I told you I would be right there if you upset her. The first trip out and she's running up the stairs in tears. I might have known."

"Oh, get out of my way."

"I don't bloody think so."

Bina sighed. "Let me go and apologise to her. I only wanted her to go on a date with him. It's normal at her age."

The shop bell clattered.

"Hardeep, do you have any change?" Kathleen Brockbank stood in the doorway.

"I'll pop up and make friends. You know me when I get an idea in my head. Perhaps I came on a bit strong."

Indecision swept through him. "One more tear, Bina. I mean it."

She pushed him through to the shop and went up the stairs as if she owned the place.

"Hi, Kathleen," he said, opening the till. "How much do you need?"

Kathleen stared over his shoulder and through the doorway. "Bina's coming and going now, is she?"

"Not invited."

Kathleen shook her head. "She always was a madam. It's a shame she didn't stay away. Twenty in ones and twenty in fifties if you've got it."

He reached into the till for some unopened change bags.

"I wouldn't disagree with on that score," he said, handing her the coins and taking the two notes she held out.

"Thanks, Hardeep."

"Kathleen, put the lock on, will you? I want to know what's going on up there."

Kathleen smiled at him. "You're a wonderful father, Hardeep. That girl is lucky to have you."

She clicked the lock and let herself out. Hardeep crept up the stairs. He hated proving Bina right, but he had good reason to snoop today. When he reached the top, his heart sunk as he heard a sob come from Satinder.

"All I'm saying is, if you don't go out with him, how do you know you don't like him?"

Always the liar, Bina had clearly carried on her matchmaking campaign.

"Sat? Is there something you're not telling me? I'm your mum. You can tell me anything."

"Mum…"

"Go on, love."

"I don't like boys. I like girls."

Hardeep thought his heart would burst out of his chest. Why on earth hadn't he seen this coming? It all made sense now.

"What did you just say?"

The sharpness in Bina's tone made him reach for the door handle.

"I like girls."

"I might have known he would bring you up to be some bloody freak."

He couldn't stand anymore and burst through the door to find Satinder crying on the chair with Bina standing over her. "What the fuck is going in here?"

"You pathetic excuse for a man. You sit there on high, making out that you're the best father in the world, and you've put ideas in her head that she's a queer."

He marched over to where they stood. "Don't you speak like that in my house. I won't have it."

"*Your* house? You wouldn't have this place if my father hadn't paid the deposit."

"Which he got back with interest."

Bina looked around the room. "No new wife though, is there? I think we all know why. If you want to know why your father and me split up, it's because I wanted a real man."

"I threw you out because you were an unfaithful tart with any man who gave you the time of day."

"Sorry for wanting a fulfilled sex life."

Satinder stood in between them.

"Stop it," she cried, before collapsing into her father's outstretched hands.

"Come on now, love. It's okay. You're okay," he soothed. "I think you should go."

"I'm not going anywhere. We have to talk about this. I'm not having any daughter of mine wandering around with rainbows all over her."

Satinder pushed Hardeep away. "I'm not your daughter. Not really. You didn't give a shit about me all this time."

Bina turned to Hardeep. "Are you going to let her speak to me like this?"

Hardeep nodded. "I certainly am."

"I won't stay where I'm not wanted," she said, making no effort to move.

"Then go," Satinder said quietly.

Bina moved towards her, but Satinder flinched and returned to the safety of Hardeep's outstretched arms. "I said go," she sobbed.

Bina stormed out of the room, letting the door slam behind her.

Hardeep had known it would end like this, but even for Bina, this had to be a record. He gently guided his daughter over to the sofa and sat her down. "I know who you need," he said, going over and opening his bedroom door. Beeb came flying out and ran straight to Satinder.

"At least he loves me." She sniffed, picking him up.

Hardeep sat on the arm of the sofa. He gently stroked her hair. "You daft bugger, I love you more than anything. Let's get things into perspective here."

"Even after what I said?"

"Talk to me, love."

"I thought you would disown me. That's why I didn't say anything."

Beeb snuffled into her neck and as Hardeep stared down, he could still see the rambunctious seven-year-old who used to fly through the place like a cyclone. She was still there.

"I couldn't disown you any more than I could disown my leg. How long have you known?"

Satinder sniffed. "All my life really."

They sat in silence for a minute, taking in the huge news that had been forced out of her.

"Dad?"

"Yes, love?"

"What did Mum mean when she said about why you split up?"

Hardeep knew what he had to say.

"Okay, you've been brave enough to talk to me. Your mother was right in a way. You're not the only person who is gay in this family."

Satinder sat up, her head twisted round. "What do you mean?"

"Sat, I'm gay too."

There it was, out in the open. The secret he had been carrying around with him all his life. Confusion spread across her face.

"You?"

"Yes."

For a second, he watched her take in the news.

"It's your fault."

She got up off the sofa, placing Beeb down on the sofa.

"What do you mean?"

"Mum was right. It's because of you I'm like this."

"Sat—"

She started to go towards her bedroom, but Hardeep took hold of her arm. "Don't go. We need to talk about things."

"It's all because of you why I don't have a mother. You always said she left, but you forced her to go. I don't blame her for going."

Satinder stopped and turned. "Your friends. I bet they're more than that, aren't they?"

Hardeep didn't know what to do. The conversation had turned down a road he hadn't expected. "Well, yes, but—"

"I don't want to hear any more. You make me sick."

She ran into her bedroom, slamming the door behind her, leaving Hardeep sitting on the sofa arm. That had been a huge mistake. Why had he hijacked her moment to talk about himself? The temptation had been too great, and he had ruined everything.

He went over to the door and knocked. "Satinder. Please come out."

Her music started playing, telling him firmly that she had no intention of talking anymore tonight. Hardeep let the tears flow. Things were out of his control now. By telling Satinder, his mother would surely find out, and that meant the rest of the village soon after. Panic overwhelmed him. Bina would be sure to capitalise on this moment and he could see him losing his daughter.

He had a sleepless night that night. Lying awake in his bed, knowing his confused and upset daughter was just the other side of the wall, pained him. He desperately wanting to scoop her up in his arms and make everything all right, but he couldn't.

The next morning, she ate her cereal in silence. Relieved that she hadn't run away in the night, he feared broaching the subject again. "What time are you at school?"

"Not until ten," she muttered.

"I need to go to work but tonight I want to talk about this. Will you come straight home?"

She sighed. "Yes."

His heart leapt a little. She hadn't completely closed the door on him. "I love you, you know."

It hurt that she couldn't look at him. "Satinder?"

"I love you too."

"Really?"

Putting her spoon down, she got up. "I'd better take Beeb for a walk."

"Wow, now I know I'm getting the cold shoulder."

How he missed the big toothless grins of that uncomplicated six-year-old. Fifteen-year-olds with their complex emotions were a lot harder to deal with.

"You need to get on your rounds. I'll see you later."

"Okay, love."

As he sorted out the parcels and letters, he saw that he needed to make a delivery to Andrew. Glancing at the clock showed him it was just after eight. Andrew didn't usually leave for work until gone nine. If he moved quickly enough, he could get up there and see how the land lay. He wanted to talk to someone desperately about the situation with Sat, but he also needed to check on the still very silent Andrew.

Anxiety rattled around in him as he made his way up the lane. Tonight he had to let Satinder know the truth of what had happened. She might not like hearing everything, but he would not let Bina rewrite history like this. He just hoped it would be in time.

Even though he could easily just put the letter through the letterbox, he knocked.

He didn't get an answer.

He knocked again, harder this time. Sally started barking upstairs. Andrew never went anywhere without her. He had to be in.

"Andrew?"

Still nothing.

Andrew's car was in the drive to the side of the house so he couldn't have gone very far. Sally scratched at the window upstairs. Fear gripped him. Then he thought he heard a voice.

"Andrew? Are you okay?," he called.

Suddenly the door was pulled open and a man Hardeep didn't recognise stood in front of him. It was definitely the man from the pub that Will had been concerned about.

"Can I help you?"

"I have a letter for Andrew, but he needs to sign for it. Is he in?"

"No, he's gone out. I'll sign for it."

The man held his hand out expectantly.

"I can't do that. It has to be Andrew. I'll come back later."

The man didn't even reply but slammed the door shut in Hardeep's face before he could get a glimpse into the room. Something was terribly wrong. He turned and ran down the lane as fast as his legs would carry him.

Chapter Twenty-Seven

Will settled his father into the chair by the fire. Titus hadn't left Matthew's side since they'd got back that morning.

"Can I get you anything?"

"I wondered if you would do me a favour?" Matthew said.

"Of course."

"Could you ring Alistair McLure?"

Will frowned. "The estate agents in Holton? Why?"

"Because we're putting this place on the market. You are making such a sacrifice for me, so the least I can do is meet you halfway."

Sinking down on the sofa, Will stared in astonishment at Matthew. It had been quite the twenty-four hours in their lives. "Are you sure? Perhaps you should think about it. I thought it was just the shock of the fall last night."

Matthew shook his head. "After you left, I spent hours staring up at the ceiling of that godawful ward. I kept playing over in my mind what you said. I would be leaving you with a millstone around your neck. I want you to take some of your inheritance now and talk to James about buying into The King's."

"But…"

"Don't interrupt. If you can establish your name there, why not become a brand? Will Johnstone at The Sheep Inn at Holton, Will Johnstone at The Rose and Crown in Bretherstall. You could really make it round here."

His father had it all figured out and for once in his life Will didn't want to rage and rebel against his ideas. "I like it."

Matthew seemed relieved. "I was worried you would think I was taking over your life again."

Tourism was the main market for Napthwaite, and tastes had changed. People wanted upmarket decent food instead of the deep-fried rubbish he seemed to be surrounded with. He could ride this wave and become the name in this part of Yorkshire.

"It's a wonderful idea, but I told James to find someone permanent. He's already started putting feelers out."

Matthew stroked Titus' ear. "Then there's not a moment to lose, is there?"

"I don't want to leave you alone."

"I promise I won't move from this chair."

"Honestly?"

"Honestly. You'll only be half an hour and I have everything I need right here." He stared down at Titus.

Will threw another log on the fire. "Thank you, Dad. I think this is going to be a wonderful time in our lives."

"I think you might be right, son."

Will had to bolt out of the room as the tears he'd been holding back would be contained no longer. They might be on a new level now, but he didn't think his father would be able to cope with such a wanton outpouring of emotion just yet.

He threw his coat on and set off down the drive. Titus would have to be taken out, but later. As he walked up the road, the village somehow looked different to him. Instead of a place of the past, it had become a place of his future. Ange would be upset, but she would have to understand.

He wondered what Hardeep and Andrew would think. They probably wouldn't be able to pick up where they had left off. Hardeep had made it clear he wanted to focus on his family and Andrew seemed terrified of a one-on-one arrangement.

Will didn't feel ready to dive in with anyone else. No, the next few months would be all about work. James' face would be a picture when he announced this. A few months ago, Matthew Johnstone was trying to force them all out of the village and now he was going to help him build a business to be proud of. Life could have some funny twists and turns.

Once he got to the green, he stopped in his tracks. Hardeep approached him at speed and had panic all over his face. All thoughts of going to the pub evaporated as Will waited for him to approach.

"What on earth's the matter?" Will said. "You look like you've seen a ghost."

Hardeep dumped his bag of post on the ground next to them. "It's Andrew," he gasped.

"What about him?"

"We haven't heard from him since last night..."

"That's not surprising. It got a bit heavy, didn't it?"

Hardeep shook his head. "I thought that but when I delivered his letters, Sally was upstairs barking her head off but no sign of him."

"Perhaps Lisa came over and they nipped out in her car. He might have been more upset than we realised."

Hardeep shook his head. "When I knocked, a man answered. It was the guy from the pub. I'm worried."

"It's probably some guy of Lisa's. Wait. I have her number," Will said. He'd been arranging a tasting of her beer for the batter he was perfecting for the menu. He quickly found it in his contacts and connected the call.

"Hello?"

"Hi, Lisa. It's Will Johnstone from Napthwaite."

"Oh, hello. Are you ringing me because you want my beer or have you finally shagged my best friend to death?"

"You're not with him then?"

He glanced at Hardeep, who had worry etched over his face.

"No, why?" Her voice was all business now.

"We're a bit concerned about him. His ex has been in touch. Did he tell you?"

"No."

"Hardeep was delivering his post and it didn't seem right. Have you heard from Andrew today? There was a guy at his place. He told Hardeep that Andrew was out. I wanted to check he wasn't with you before we go up there, accusing people of things."

"I haven't heard from him since last week. I'm coming over."

"Okay, listen. Meet us at my dad's house. He's not well and I don't like to leave him too long."

"Thorpe Hall?"

"That's the one. There's a key under the brick to the left of the door."

Will cut the call and texted his father. He didn't want him having a relapse when a stranger came in. "Come on," he said to Hardeep.

They set off the way Hardeep had come. As they got to the bus stop by the school, they saw Satinder waiting.

"Dad?" she said, glancing at Will. "Is everything all right?"

Hardeep put his bag down next to her. "Can you keep hold of this for a bit?"

"But I'm going to school."

Hardeep glanced at Will. "Listen, Sat, you'll have to be late. We think Andrew's ex is here and he's not a nice person. Will and I are going to check on him."

Panic spread across her face. She grabbed her dad's sleeve. "I don't want you to go. He might be dangerous."

Hardeep gently removed her fingers from his jacket and kissed the back of her hand. "I'll be okay. There's two of us. Do me a favour and take the bag to the shop. Dean is working in half an hour. He can keep it safe and tell him if anyone complains about getting their post late, it's an emergency."

But Satinder wouldn't be dissuaded. "I mean it, Dad. I don't want anything to happen to you. I love you too much."

He threw his arms around her and held her close. The tenderness between them made Will's heart melt. Hardeep truly was a special man.

"Nothing will happen to me. I love you too, but I love Will and Andrew as well. I have to go. Tell me you understand."

Hearing Hardeep declare his love for the two of them felt strange. But in that moment of peril, Will knew that he felt exactly the same. He had for months. Nothing would stop him from going to make sure Andrew was safe.

"You love them?" Satinder asked, wide-eyed.

"Yes, I really do."

Satinder looked at Will. "I hope you love him too."

The ferocity in which she said this took him aback. "Oh, I do. More than he will ever know."

Satinder took this in for a second. "Go then," she said. "But I'm not going to school and worrying about you. What do you need me to do?"

Will wanted to get moving. They needed to get this sorted and quickly. "Go to check on my dad, please. Lisa, Andrew's friend, is on her way but I don't like to leave him. He was in hospital last night with a fall. Don't let him get out of his chair."

She nodded. "Mr Johnstone has always scared me a bit."

"You and me both." Will laughed. "But he's a pussycat if you make a decent cup of tea."

Hardeep pulled her in for another hug. "She makes the best tea, which is surprising because she never gets any practice."

She squirmed out of his grip and picked up the bag. "Hurry," she said. With that she set off down towards the green.

"You ready?" Will asked Hardeep.

"Abso-fucking-lutely," he replied.

Chapter Twenty-Eight

They were nearly falling over each other as they made their way up the lane. Hardeep's heart hammered as they got to the gate. Just as Will put his hand on it, Hardeep stopped him.

"Wait. That gate makes a racket. We don't want them to know we're here. Not until we check out what the hell is going on."

Will looked at him impatiently. "What do we do then?"

"Do it quietly. Here."

Hardeep pushed the gate slowly. He winced as it made a slight grinding noise but eventually it opened. "They were in the living room when I came before," he whispered. "If we crawl under the windowsill, we should be able to get the lay of the land. They might be having a brew, and we'll look like idiots."

"I don't think so. If it was Neil in the pub last night, he seems like a nasty bastard," Will replied.

"I'm scared," Hardeep said without thinking.

Will kissed him softly on the lips. "So am I but we have to do this. We love him, remember?"

"We love each other."

Will nodded. "And it's about time we did something about it."

No more words were necessary so they both crawled along the garden path. A flower bed backed onto the wall, and they had to move through Andrew's prized display. *He won't be very happy with this.*

Once they had got into position, Hardeep could barely breathe. Everything seemed deafening to his heightened senses.

Will nodded. Hardeep nodded too and slowly they raised their heads. It seemed to take so long as they cleared the windowsill. The adrenalin had got to almost unbearable levels as Hardeep's eyes cleared the sill and he started to make out the inside of the house.

It took a second for his eyes to become accustomed, but what he saw made him almost cry out. There was blood on the walls. Frantically he scanned the rest of the room. His gaze rested on the prone figure of Andrew, lying on the floor. The shirt he had on was soaked in blood and in tatters at the back. To Hardeep's relief, he saw Andrew twitch. He was alive and awake. That had to be a good thing.

Every instinct in him wanted to barge the door down and get to him, but he saw the figure on the chair, looking over Andrew. It had to be Neil. In his hand he held a big knife that Hardeep did not fancy getting on the wrong side of.

In unison, they slowly lowered themselves down. Hardeep didn't want Neil to see any movement out of the corner of his eye. Will pointed to the gate.

With movements as imperceptible as they could manage, they retraced their steps. Hardeep got through to the lane, but Will's coat caught on the gate making it swing back, giving a high-pitched squeak.

Suddenly Sally's face appeared at one of the upstairs window, and she started barking like crazy when she saw them.

In the nick of time, Hardeep and Will scuttled behind Andrew's car. To Hardeep's horror the front door opened and footsteps scrunched the gravel on the path. The gate made another noise and Hardeep ducked down farther. From where he was, he could see feet on the other side of the car. Holding his breath, Hardeep wished he could get into the house and lock the door, but the knife he felt sure Neil had in his hand would stop him in his tracks.

Sally barked as loudly as possible. Neil's feet turned and he walked up to the house.

"I'm going to slit her fucking throat if she makes any more noise," he said as he slammed the door shut.

Will and Hardeep both exhaled.

"Fucking hell, I'm not cut out for this," Will said, rubbing his chest.

Hardeep rummaged in his pockets.

"What are you doing?" Will whispered.

"What I should have done in the first place," he said, putting his phone to his ear. "Police, quickly."

The operator put him through, and he explained the situation as best he could to the person on the other end of the line.

"Police?"

Hardeep fought the tears threatening to overwhelm him. "Hello, yes. My friend is trapped inside his house with a man with a knife."

"Tell them his name. They might know him," Will urged.

"His name is Andrew Norris. His ex-boyfriend is abusive. Please hurry. We looked in the window and he's been slashed with a knife."

"And they don't know you're there?" the call handler said.

"No," Hardeep still whispered. "He came out but has gone inside now. Send someone quickly."

"They are already on the way. Do not approach and wait for the officers to arrive. I will stay on the line with you."

"Okay," Hardeep said.

Will looked like he had other ideas.

"Are they coming?" he asked.

Hardeep nodded.

"Terminate the call then."

Hardeep frowned. He wasn't sure what Will had in mind.

"Quickly. I've an idea."

He did as Will said and put his phone in his pocket. "What are you playing at?"

Will glanced over the bonnet of Andrew's car. "You're still in your uniform. If you go and knock on the door, say you've a letter needs to be signed for, it will distract that bastard."

"And what are you going to do?"

"I'll go in through the garage. It will be the last thing he's expecting."

Hardeep was no hero and he shared Will's desperation to get Andrew out of there, but this was a mad plan.

"We should just wait for the police. They will know what to do."

"Hardeep, we live in the middle of nowhere. They will take ages. The ambulance was over an hour for dad last night. He'll either kill Andrew, Sally or both of them. Come on."

Will scrambled to his feet and made his way into the garage. Hardeep knew he would do this with or without his help and he stood a far better chance if he provided a distraction.

Trying to focus his fear, he set off towards the gate.

"Slowly," Will said. "Act natural."

Swallowing his fear down, Hardeep opened the gate and wandered down the path as normally as he could muster. He didn't look into the window as he wanted to and stopped at the door that Neil had slammed shut only moments ago.

He knocked on the door. *Keep calm, Hardeep. It's just a normal day on your round.*

There was no answer, but he hadn't expected there to be.

"Andrew, it's Hardeep. I've a letter here for you, needs signing for."

Movement could be heard in the garage. Will would be making his way inside the house. He could almost pass out with the tension.

Knocking again, he made it louder this time, desperate to drown out the tiniest of noises. "Andrew. Are you in, mate? Sally's going mad up there. Is everything all right?"

Suddenly all hell broke loose. Through the frosted glass of the door window, he saw door inside fling open and what looked like bodies colliding. Without thinking, Hardeep pushed open the door. Will and Neil were in the middle of the room, fighting over the knife.

Hardeep rushed over to Andrew, slipping and falling. He grasped hold of him to try to get him to safety but there was no shifting him. Andrew cried out in pain as he pulled hard.

Will and Neil crashed over the sofa and onto the floor by the fireplace. Neil pushed Will away and slashed at his arm. Blood spattered up the white walls and Will screamed in pain. He collapsed onto the coffee table and Neil stood. He towered over Will.

"I don't know who the fuck you are, but I'm going to finish the lot of you."

Sally was throwing herself against the stair door. Hardeep ran to it and released her into the room. Maybe it was all the pent-up energy of being shut upstairs for hours or the fact that her master's life lay on the line, but Sally knew exactly what to do.

She darted across the room and spring-boarded off the upended sofa. She hit Neil square in the neck, biting at him with her snapping mouth. The weight of the dog sent him crashing to the floor, with a sickening thud. The knife flew out of his grip and Hardeep dove for it as though he were a top-class rugby player.

Will struggled to his feet and dragged Sally away before she could do any serious damage to Neil. As it stood, he had bite marks on his face but she had merely played with him.

Neil tried to get up, but Will kicked him back down.

"Don't fucking move."

Chapter Twenty-Nine

They were all crowded in Matthew's book-lined study. The night had started to draw in and Will had banked the fire up.

It had all been a blur once the emergency services turned up.

"I still think they should have taken you in," Matthew muttered.

"It's just a surface wound, Dad. Honestly, I can hardly feel it."

That probably had a lot to do with the industrial-strength pain relief they had given him. The paramedic had wanted him to get checked over, but Will had refused. He had wanted to get back to see his father. Not that he would tell him that.

Poor Hardeep had been torn with what to do. Andrew had lost some blood, but the paramedics had thought it looked worse than it was.

"You'd be surprised how blood can travel," one of them had cheerfully announced as they loaded Andrew's stretcher onto the ambulance.

Reluctantly, they had watched the vehicle drive off. The next thing had been facing endless questions from the police. Mercifully that had happened once they'd got to Thorpe Hall. As soon as Lisa had heard what had happened, she'd set off for the hospital at top speed.

"I'm sick of all this bloody waiting," Satinder exclaimed. She got a flick across the head from her father, who she had been stuck to like glue ever since he'd walked through the door.

"Enough of the language, thank you."

"I get it from you," she said.

Hardeep shrugged at Will. "What am I going to do with her?"

"Spoil her rotten and cuddle her as much as possible?" he suggested.

Hardeep complied and pulled his daughter closer.

They all gave a start when car lights lit up the room.

"That's them," Satinder said, jumping to her feet.

Matthew struggled to get up, but Will swept in and gently put his hand on his arm.

"Not so fast," he said with a smile.

His father huffed and sat in his chair. "I'm not completely useless. I can answer my own door, you know."

"But I do it with so much more grace," he replied.

A twinkle appeared in Matthew's eyes. "Go on then."

Will dashed through to the hallway and opened the door. Andrew had already made it onto the step and fell into his arms. Will hugged him tight until he cried out. "Mind my back," he exclaimed.

"Oh, he's got more stitches in there than a bloody wedding dress," Lisa said, following him.

Will ushered them into the study. "Can you sit down?" he asked.

Andrew gingerly lowered himself onto the chair by the desk. "Sleeping is going to be fun," he said miserably.

"You'll all stay here tonight," Matthew announced.

"All of us?" Satinder asked.

Matthew nodded. "We've enough room. Might as well make the most of it. You ladies can have the twin room. Hardeep, you can have the Green Room, and Andrew can have the Octagon Room."

Will glanced across at the other two. Hardeep nodded to him.

"Dad. You do know that Hardeep, Andrew and I are together, don't you?"

The older man looked from one to the other in turn. "You mean like those three at The King's?"

"Kind of, Mr Johnstone," said Hardeep. "But we want it to remain private. There's no need for any fuss."

Matthew fiddled with the edging of the blanket that covered his legs, seemingly deep in thought. "Well, I suppose anyone can sleep where they bloody well like then," he said, eventually. "I don't understand you young folk. Since when did one person stop being enough?"

"Oh, it's more than enough for me, Mr J," Lisa piped up. "It's just these greedy boys. Now I distinctly remember you telling me about a whisky collection when we were waiting before?"

Matthew's whisky collection was under lock and key in a big cabinet by his desk. He turned to Will. "You'd better get the key, son. We've a few nerves to calm tonight."

"It's in the kitchen. I'll get it," Will said.

He started to make his way to the door when Andrew got up. "Hardeep, I think we need to all have a chat."

Satinder gripped her father's arm. "Can I come?"

Hardeep seemed torn for a second. They needed a moment together, but that girl had had the shock of her life and standing in the way of her and her father would not be the way to start things off.

Matthew came to the rescue. "Satinder, why don't you finish the Chapter of that book you were reading to me before? We were just getting to an exciting bit, and I'll never sleep unless we get to the end."

He winked at Will, who felt a rush of love for the man. He wanted to project every molecule of that feeling towards him.

Satinder sat on the floor next to Matthew's chair and fished a book out from underneath that had a bookmark in it.

Lisa plonked herself down on the sofa. "And hurry up with that whisky. If I have to listen to any more about goblins and bloody wizards, I will need a drink."

Hardeep got up and helped Andrew over to the doorway.

The fire crackled and the logs fell down a little.

"Satinder, please could you throw another one on?" Will asked.

"I've just found our place," she complained, then thought better of it and crawled over to the log basket. She selected one and threw it onto the fire.

"That's a girl," Lisa laughed. "You'll have to do as you're told from now on. You've two wicked stepmothers to boss you about."

Satinder resumed her position at Matthew's feet. "They'll be better than my real mum any day."

Will glanced at Hardeep, whose lip was trembling.

Satinder spun round and looked up at Matthew. "That makes you my step-grandfather."

The older man seemed taken aback for a second then reached down and ruffled her hair. "That it does, lass, and a proud one at that. Now come on. I want to know if they cast the spell or not."

They left the room just as Satinder started to read from the book.

In the kitchen, Sally lazed in Titus' bed. She seemed to know her newfound status as hero of the hour and had made light work of the steak that Will had defrosted for her, and all the while Titus and Beeb had watched in disgust.

Once the kitchen door swung shut, they fell on one another, sobbing. It was almost as if all the tension of the day had been held until this intimate moment.

"Again, please remember I have a shit ton of stitches," Andrew exclaimed but held them both tightly to him.

Will's tears soaked Andrew's shirt as he nestled against his chest. He held Hardeep tightly to him and they stood there for what felt like an eternity.

"Thank God," Hardeep exclaimed. "When I saw you lying on the floor, I thought —"

"Enough of that," Andrew said, kissing him. "I'm all right. I'll have a bloody good scar though. I'll tell the hot boys I got it on some adventure."

Will playfully punched him on the arm. "You'll be telling the boys nothing. Not on our watch."

Andrew sat on a kitchen stool. Hardeep and Will stood before him, their arms around each other. Andrew leant forward and took their hands.

"So we're going to do this then?"

"I don't think we can't," Will said. "Not now. I love both of you and I don't care if you get freaked out by that."

"There'll be no more freaking out. I owe you two my life. It only seems fair that I share it with you. All the way."

Will and Andrew turned to Hardeep.

"My daughter tells me I'd be a fool not to," he said.

"And what about what you think?" Will said.

"I think today my worst nightmares and best dreams have come true. How often can you say that?"

They leant forward and all three shared a kiss. Will rested his head on Hardeep's shoulder.

"I think you're right though, Hardeep. Let's not broadcast it. I don't need Mrs Turnbull picking over our every move."

"And reporting back to your mother," Andrew added.

"Oh God, my mother. I doubt very much she'll keep it to herself. We have two weeks tops."

Will smiled. "Then we make those two weeks count. Let's go for this. I mean really go for it and fuck what Mrs Turnbull, your mother or even the bloody Queen thinks."

They each took one another's hands.

"You've got yourself a deal." Hardeep grinned.

Falling into another hug, Will marvelled at how he had found paradise between these two men.

"I've lived in fear for so bloody long. I don't know what to think."

Will ran his hands through Andrew's hair while Hardeep nuzzled his neck. "You have nothing more to fear, Andrew Norris. We're a team. Forever."

"Then I will spend the rest of my life being thankful that I came to this village," he replied.

With no more words needed, they stood there, their bodies entwined. The future could wait for a little while.

Want to see more from this author? Here's a taster for you to enjoy!

Village Affairs: Triple Intent
Kristian Parker

Excerpt

Even in December, the Greek sunlight streamed through a chink in the curtains, painting the bed in heat. François Vernier stretched out in the Egyptian cotton sheets and tried to ignore the dull thud of a hangover playing in his brain. They had started the party early, yet it felt like he'd only just put his head down.

A very disorientated Darryl Burlington emerged from under the duvet with a lop-sided grin. "Merry Christmas, François."

The nausea came rapidly, and François had to lay his head on the pillow again. "*Joyeux Noel.*"

Darryl plumped his pillows and sat up. "What a night, eh?"

François nodded. "I need coffee. You want?"

Not waiting for a reply, he got out of bed and padded over to the kitchen area of the vast suite Darryl had taken where he made himself busy grinding some beans. The view down to the Ionian Sea took his breath away and once the machine bubbled into life, he took it all in.

Kefalonia was a small island on the west coast of Greece. François had been to many other Greek islands but never this one. He couldn't wait to return in the summer when it would be warm enough to dive into those blue waters. François prided himself on always being a participant and hated being a spectator.

Ever impatient, he waited until just enough coffee for two cups had brewed. Filling them, he ignored the hissing sound of more dripping onto the hot plate.

He went through to the bedroom. Darryl hadn't moved. As fresh as a daisy, he grinned at him. Darryl believed hangovers were for the weak. François didn't dare glance in the mirror that covered half a wall. But Darryl had insisted on partying into the night so he would have to take him as he found him.

"What are we doing today?" Darryl asked.

François handed him his cup and opened the curtains a little. He didn't care if anyone saw him naked. It would give them an early Christmas treat. He'd been turning heads since he'd been in his pram. His mother told him that when she'd pushed him through town, people would stop and speak to him. If they were lucky, he would reward them with a smile. Some days he wouldn't.

He blew on his coffee and took a sip. The hangover had become a little more insistent, and he regretted making quite so many plans for today. "George said he would take us out on the boat. Everywhere is closed, so I thought a picnic somewhere lovely then back here for dinner."

Darryl nodded.

François went over to his bag that lay on the chair. He rummaged inside and retrieved the gift he had kept secret. "Merry Christmas."

He handed it to a surprised Darryl. "I thought we weren't doing gifts. I haven't got you anything."

François shrugged and ignored the feeling in his heart. Darryl ripped off the paper and revealed the monogrammed leather notebook from Aspinal.

"Oh, François. I love it. Thank you."

Darryl reached out his hand for François. He sat down on the bed, and they hugged each other awkwardly.

"Ah you're awake. I thought you two were going to sleep all of Christmas Day."

François spun round to see Ezio, the Greek barman they had picked up the night before. He stood in the doorway wearing just a towel. His thick curly hair dripped water onto his furry chest, the inviting glint in his eye that had first prompted Darryl to send François over with their indecent proposal still very much in place.

"François?" Darryl said, licking his lips. "Tell George not to bother with the boat. I think we should stay at home today."

He pulled the duvet aside, letting the notebook fall to the floor. François glanced momentarily at the gift lying there before putting on his game face.

"Yes, boss. Sounds good to me."

Ezio dropped the towel, revealing the delights they had enjoyed all night long. François' cock twitched. Darryl probably had a point. A day on the high seas would only make him seasick. He walked over and kissed Ezio.

"That's right, boys," Darryl said. He put his hands behind his head, licking his lips. "Give me a Christmas show."

* * * *

Four hours later, they had moved onto champagne. Ezio had some stamina on him. François lay on the couch, sipping a glass as he listened to Darryl and Ezio going at it in the next room.

If his parents could see him now, he didn't know if they would be impressed or disgusted. Probably a mix of the two. He hadn't spoken to them in ten years so who knew?

The suite had everything he and Darryl could want. A private pool, butler—who Darryl had magnanimously given the day off—and wraparound views. His mind rested on the Christmas Days he'd had as a kid. His grandparents coming to see his new toys and playing simple games before joining the rest of the village for carols.

A tear escaped his eye which he hastily wiped away. *No use dwelling on the past.*

Draining the glass, he wandered over to the wine cooler and grabbed another bottle. There was always another when he travelled with Darryl Burlington.

He made his way over to the bedroom, to be greeted by the sight of Ezio riding Darryl's cock hard. His lithe furry body bucked in time to Darryl's grunting. François popped the cork loudly and they both stopped.

"I thought you might need some refreshment."

Ezio climbed off Darryl, pulling the condom off him and throwing it in the bin. "Sounds good to me," he replied.

Darryl hadn't left the bed yet. Why would he? Everything had been brought to him.

François poured the champagne and handed a long-stemmed crystal flute to each of the sweating men.

"What time did you say you were working, Ezio?"

Sipping his drink, the gorgeous man glanced at his watch.

"Oh shit," he exclaimed. He slammed the glass down on the bedside table. "Can I have another shower?"

"Sure," Darryl said.

Ezio brushed past François and out of the room.

"He can go on forever," Darryl grinned.

"You weren't doing so bad yourself," François replied.

At forty-two years old, Darryl Burlington was still in his prime. Sweat beaded on his dark brown skin as he took a swig of his drink. "I'm starving," he announced. "Get rid of him and we can go for dinner?"

François tried not to pout. "I thought we could order up and watch a movie."

Darryl shook his head. "Nah, that'll be boring. Let's see if there's any life going on out there. Maybe find us one last Christmas treat?" He winked at François.

"You're on heat," he said.

"It's Christmas Day." Darryl laughed. "What are we doing tomorrow?"

François walked over to the window. "George is taking us to the site in the morning. Then our flight is at two."

"Perfect. I might have a quick nap. Build my strength up."

Darryl snuggled down under the sheets. François drained his glass and walked out to the living area where Ezio had thrown on a pair of jeans.

"Do you know what happened to my T-shirt?" he said.

François took him in. Another exceptionally handsome man to add to their collection. He couldn't say he hadn't enjoyed being fucked all ways by him.

But he joined a very long line. Darryl was a hunter and soon lost interest when the quarry was captured.

François dug behind one of the sofa cushions and found a grey T-shirt. He threw it across to the gorgeous man.

"Thanks," Ezio said with a wink. "I had a really great time."

"Yeah, me too," François said.

He always had to the get rid of them. No matter how many people they invited to the room, François assumed the role of doorman. They would always want more, and he would have to let them down gently. Darryl probably didn't even know this dance was done after he'd had his pleasure.

"Do you want to tell your face that?" Ezio said.

"Huh?"

"It's Christmas Day, François. You look as though you're going to the dentist."

François smiled. "Sorry. Been working hard lately."

Pulling the shirt over his head, Ezio came over and wrapped his arms around François' waist. He ignored the instinct to push him away.

"Now you've played hard. It's the best medicine." Ezio kissed him. "Should I say goodbye to Darryl?"

François shook his head. "Best not. He's getting some shut-eye before we get to do it all again."

"Call in at the bar?" Ezio asked hopefully.

François nodded vaguely. Darryl didn't believe in lightning striking twice, so they wouldn't be going in that bar again.

"Sure. Now go to work," he said. He extracted himself from Ezio's arms and walked over to the hallway. "I'm going to finish that bottle and find a trashy Christmas movie to watch."

But Ezio didn't move. "Why don't you just be with him?"

François stopped in his tracks. "I'm sorry?"

"Darryl. It's obvious you're in love with him."

Tension ran through François' body. Ezio wasn't the first to say this, but the question always made him defensive. It must be crystal clear for people on the outside. "It's not that like that. Darryl and I are complicated."

Ezio made a face. "I can't see how. When I've gone, go in there and fuck his brains out. Then tell him you love him."

François dashed over to the open bedroom door. The room lay in darkness, but surely Darryl couldn't have dropped off that quickly. He did not want him overhearing this stranger dissecting a relationship they had never bothered to define in eight years. He gently shut the door.

"Firstly, we only play with others. Secondly, I'm not in love with anyone, thank you. Thirdly, if I were I wouldn't be discussing it with a stranger. Got that?"

Realising he would have to be way more forthright, he marched over to the main door. Opening it with purpose, he wanted to make it perfectly clear this experience had come to an end. But Ezio wasn't so easily put off. He stopped by François, his face so close that François could smell the stale alcohol on him.

"Will you return to Kefalonia?"

"Probably," François said. "We're thinking of buying a place in the south. I will come for the opening."

"Then get in touch."

"Darryl probably won't come. He doesn't bother these days."

"I don't care. I'd like to see you again."

This man had outstayed his welcome. His overconfident manner grated on François. "Sure, whatever. Find me on Insta. François Vernier."

Ezio nodded and kissed him before leaving the suite. François shut the door behind him. He did not need to be psychoanalysed by a one-night stand on Christmas Day. *When did meaningless sex become such hard work?*

Resisting the temptation to crawl in beside Darryl, he sat down on the couch and poured himself another glass of champagne. He didn't blame Ezio for being envious that he lived the high life in suites like this, but he wouldn't let some scheming barman overstep the mark. He had spent the last few years being everything Darryl needed. He knew what he wanted before Darryl did. Darryl often joked that he was more of a husband than an assistant. At night when he was alone in bed, François would think about what it would be like if they were real partners.

We could rule the world.

About the Author

I have written for as long as I could write. In fact, before, when I would dictate to my auntie. I love to read, and I love to create worlds and characters.

I live in the English countryside. When I'm not writing, I like to get out there and think through the next scenario I'm going to throw my characters into.

Inspiration can be found anywhere, on a train, in a restaurant or in an office. I am always in search of the next character to find love in one of my stories. In a world of apps and online dating, it is important to remember love can be found when you least expect it.

Kristian loves to hear from readers. You can find his contact information, website details and author profile page at https://www.pride-publishing.com

PUBLISHING

Sign up for our newsletter and find out about all our
romance book releases, eBook sales and promotions,
sneak peeks and FREE romance books!